I0587067

HE WAS BEEB WHEN I KNEW HIM

RENOIR

He Was BEEB When I Knew Him

Copyright © 2022 Renoir

All rights reserved.

Print ISBN: 978-0-6489413-6-1

E-book ISBN: 978-0-6489413-7-8

*Published by **Meredian Pictures & Words** 2022*

Ballina, Australia

No parts of this publication may be reproduced, stored in a retrieval system, or transmitted in any form or by any means, electronic, mechanical, photocopying, recording, or otherwise, without the prior written permission of the copyright owner.

This book is sold subject to the condition that it shall not, by way of trade or otherwise, be lent, resold, hired out, or otherwise circulated without the publisher's prior consent in any form of binding or cover other than that in which it is published and without a similar condition including this condition being imposed on the subsequent purchaser. Under no circumstances may any part of this book be photocopied for resale.

This is a work of fiction. Any similarity between the characters and situations within its pages and places or persons, living or dead, is unintentional and co-incidental.

❀ Created with Vellum

*With thanks to Brian and Earle, wherever they are,
and to my Muse and darling bride.*

CONTENTS

BOYHOOD

1

BEGINNINGS

I'd known Beeb for a couple of years before I actually knew him. I mean, I'd seen him around the school, but for a while he was just one of the mob. It was one of Brisbane's modestly self-proclaimed Greater Public Schools - all male, everyone with regulation haircuts and matching uniforms. You only really knew the ones you shared a class with.

For the first three years of High School classes were divided according to which language you'd chosen to study in Grade 8. During my primary school years, I'd read enough issues of *Commando Action* comics to think I had a pretty fair grasp of German (I knew "achtung" and "himmel!") so that had been my choice. I'd also watched enough episodes of *Hogan's Heroes* to reckon that I had a handle on the accent.

Beeb had elected to study French, because he liked their food, I later discovered. It came as a bonus to him to develop an interest in French philosophy and culture. He was fascinated by sophistication before most blokes could spell the word.

It wasn't until our second last year of school that I found myself studying English alongside Brandon Baxter Bowmore (B. B. B. - Beeb, get it?)

Nicknames were commonplace in the school. Not everyone had one, but a clear majority were so endowed. That was to be expected in an environment where there were so many instances of similar names. One of my classes included six Johns, two Jons, a Jan and a Johann. Teachers normally overcame this by addressing boys by their surnames, adding an initial or two if there were, for instance, multiple Smiths in a class.

There was something subtly dehumanizing about being called out as 'Wilson', 'McCafferty' or 'Jones, G. K.'. Better than being just a number, but when you'd spent your whole life answering to your Christian name (forename, if you prefer, or if your faith is perturbed by the old-fashioned terminology) the change took a bit of getting used to. And it could generate its own confusions. One class had a "Gregory, G." and a "Gregory, W." in addition to two blokes who'd actually been christened Gregory. One of them was Greg Williams – luckily "Gregory, W." knew himself as 'Bill', or the confusion would have been worse.

Amongst ourselves we coined nicknames as a more genial alternative. Very few blokes got to choose their own epithet. Something like "Call me Butch," had next to no chance of working. Most commonly, the names were descriptors of some sort of physical characteristic or mannerism, or the twisting of a surname. They weren't always flattering, but you didn't have much choice other than to get used to it.

A few examples: 'Tree' and 'Peewee', who were the tallest and shortest guys in our year respectively; 'Wingnut', for his prominent ears; 'Shades', who wore medically-prescribed tinted glasses; 'Goggles' whose specs held very thick lenses; 'Tweeter', whose unusually high voice never did seem to break; 'Spider', surnamed Webb (his older brother missed that because his extreme unattractiveness had immediately prompted 'Ugly'); 'Alice' Cooper and 'Pink' Floyd; and 'B.O.', for distressingly obvious reasons that also coincidentally played on his given name, which I'll diplomatically record as Bruce Oliver to protect his true identity.

'Ace' Martin and 'Mazaire' Morgan got their names in the course of the card games that were hugely popular before school and during lunch. 'Firetruck' Jones had chosen that particular word to replace the four-letter expletive he got in strife for using too freely, and used it so often it stuck as a nickname.

There were of course also the simple, classically Aussie contractions like Ando, Thommo and Johnno.

I was dubbed 'Paddy' due to confusion over the ethnic origins of my vestigial Scottish accent. There was a TV commercial getting much airplay at the time which featured a garrulous Irish potato farmer called Paddy. The cloth ears of some of my classmates couldn't distinguish between his accent and the Glaswegian burr I'd inherited. Given that heritage, my parents were understandably unimpressed by my new nickname. But it was never used at home, and despite my initial misgivings I quickly got used to it around school and my mates.

In turn, I took some credit for coming up with Beeb's soubriquet - one that he accepted willingly. It replaced the short-lived 'Frenchy' (bestowed because he got the accent exactly right in his very first French class) which was quickly realised to be more apt for another of his classmates whose own name was far more from the left bank of the Seine – Charles Chevalier.

It would be overstating things to call Beeb handsome. Striking is a better word. A square jaw and alabaster paleness gave his face a sculpted look, comparatively uncluttered by the red ravages of pimples and acne that bedevilled most of us. I remember one stubborn recurring spot of my own which parked just above the bridge of my nose like a mystic's third eye. If I'd been Indian I might have gotten away with painting the wretched thing black.

The whiteness of his skin was offset by thick, jet-black eyebrows and hair. The same combination as Disney's *Snow White*. It should have made him a prime candidate for sunburn and eventual skin cancer, but he was one of the few in the school who regularly wore the broad-brimmed hat that was only an optional part of our uniform. It always seemed strange in Brisbane's climate that hats were optional and ties compulsory.

Beeb was just over average height, and enjoyed a nice, even growth rate that kept him at or near that median all the way through his school years. Unlike some of us, whose growth pattern traced an irregular series of explosive bursts amid fallow spells of inconstant length.

Neither did he gain or lose the disproportionate amount of weight that made life awkward for some of our peers. One guy got progressively skinnier over his time at school until he spent his final year there known to all as 'Scarecrow'. 'Lump' Graham went from overweight to obese to a point where his nickname became 'House' because he was as big as one. 'Cowboy' Byron's shape fluctuated from year to year, term to term even, between flabby, well-built and lean, and back again. Maybe his mother produced wildly different meals according to the season, or maybe his metabolism, appetite or activities just varied a lot.

Beeb had the sort of solid build that might soon turn to fat but for his predilection for walking long distances. He came to school by bus, and left the same way. But on the way home he would often get off several stops early, and walk home in peaceful, contemplative solitude. As he got older, the length of those walks grew. So too did his disregard for inclement weather.

This created a problem one afternoon when his briefcase turned out to be less waterproof than he'd assumed. Three assignments in various stages of near-completion were ruined by the rain. A couple of all-night sessions were apparently required for them to be reconstructed and completed on time. The experience might have dissuaded someone else from walking home in the rain. Beeb took to keeping plastic bags in his case, ready to wrap assignments and other important paperwork in if the weather required it.

It didn't take long for me to realise that here was a guy whose perspective on the world was a little different. Even in an English class that featured a greater-than-average number of eccentric characters (good and bad) he stood out.

He seemed quiet and sort of bookwormish. The term 'nerd' wasn't in common currency yet. He appeared the sort of bloke who you'd expect to be an academic whiz and a social misfit. In fact, he *was* something of an academic whiz, and very much a misfit, but that latter was more by design than social ineptitude. He liked to exercise his mind and imagination, and liked provoking others into doing the same. That was a combination sure to alienate him from many blokes who were either plodding through their sentences at school or already single-mindedly pursuing a chosen career path to professional riches in law or medicine. (Chosen by them or family.)

Our English teacher in Grades 11 and 12 was an earnest and wryly witty Welshman named Earle Seccombe. He was well equipped to deal with eccentric characters. I strongly suspect he'd been one during his own school days. I knew he was respected in the teachers' common room, but I'd also seen and heard that not everyone there appreciated him. Mavericks were no more encouraged among the staff than among the students, and Earle had been obliged to mostly master the art of visible diplomacy.

He wasn't especially ambitious. He had a good position at a prestigious school, thanks very much, could he now be left alone to enjoy encouraging young minds to share his enthusiasm for our language, please? Of course not. There was a Curriculum to be adhered to, and school policy. Managerial-style 'performance indicators' hadn't yet been introduced for teachers, but everyone on staff knew that the objective was to cram as many of the school's students into the top echelon of Tertiary Education entrants as possible. That was the yardstick by which school fees could be set. 'Academic excellence' it was called.

When presented with our class, Earle knew he'd been given what he called "a bag of all-sorts". He did look at everyone's previous academic results, and not just in English. And he apparently did quietly consult with other teachers. But he was shrewd enough to listen and observe, and reach his own conclusions about his pupils.

The 'all-sorts' description was pretty apt, although we mostly fell into one of two broad categories. At one extreme were those who were in an English class only because it was compulsory. They could speak the language, or their local variant of it, and wanted no more than that. Literature peaked at the *Farmers' Gazette*. The closest thing to poetry was a crude limerick about the Bishop of Buckingham.

At the other end of the spectrum were those boys who 'got' English. As a means of communication and expression, conveying ideas and emotions and images. Making facts and information clear, making concepts comprehensible, making the fanciful realistic.

Consequently, members of Earle's class sat at either end of the results table. Few ever actually failed (it wasn't an option at our school) but some routinely scraped pass marks by knowing, and doing, just enough. Also among our number were four of our year's top five English students, and some more who weren't far behind.

That combination allowed Earle to discreetly tick all the boxes on the 'prescribed reading list' much earlier in a term than teachers of other classes. The bright ones caught on quickly and finished the required work without too much difficulty. Those on the other side of the balance wouldn't achieve better than their usual disinterested mediocrity with three times as much teaching, so compressing the process did no harm, either.

This meant that for the later weeks of each term we could pursue things dearer to Earle's heart. Monty Python, and why the show was funny. Ditto the Goon Show. Why was some science fiction uncannily prophetic while some remained completely implausible? If rock music was the poetry of our generation, who would be remembered in two hundred years, and why?

In those weeks our English class was more like a discussion group. Young minds were challenged, and most revelled in it. Even among the comparative underachievers, interest was often piqued and insights sometimes came from unlikely sources. Over Grades 11 and 12 several of the 'dead end kids' steadily improved their marks to levels nobody, including their families, had expected

For three years we'd been force fed the conventional diet of Dickens and Shakespeare and the recognized Literary Greats. Even potentially interesting writers like Tolkein and Coleridge had lost their appeal by a process of study that parsed their work down and dried it out. The answer to "Why did he write this?" was never, "For the sheer pleasure of it". Thus, we were robbed of the joy of their creativity – everything had to have A Meaning. Earle Seccombe's approach brought back some pleasure in the written word. Too late to save Dickens, Conrad or James Joyce for me, I'm afraid, but there were other writers who I could still appreciate.

Among our Grade II English textbooks was Herman Hesse's brush with Indian mysticism and mythology *Siddhartha* - an esoteric choice even for the early 1970's. It was fairly early in our time together, and I don't think Earle yet had high hopes of what such an unconventional challenge might provoke.

With an "Oh well, it's in the syllabus" sigh Earle gave the class the assignment of analyzing the book. Most of the group produced their usual lifeless recyclings of various commentaries by Distinguished Literary Critics. This was an approach that had been accepted, encouraged even, over the previous years of English classes. It required little or no independent thought, and produced little or no genuine insight. It wasn't learning, it was process. It suited the unimaginative clods, and had become an easy routine for many of the brighter pupils. But Earle had suggested that he wanted something more.

I achieved some notoriety with an assignment that set out to reveal Herman's book as a protracted endorsement of the use of mind-altering drugs. I did it well enough to get the second-best mark in the class.

Top of the class was Beeb, who had interpreted the journeyings and experiences of Hesse's lead character Siddhartha as a "remark-able prophetic allegory of the life and work of George Harrison". He had supported his assertion with finesse, drawing detailed parallels between the novel and the biography and lyrical/musical catalogue to that point of the former Beatles' guitarist.

Earle was, fortunately, a teacher of sufficient wisdom to mark essays on merit, not whether he agreed with the writers' conclusions. Furthermore, I suspect that he was so fed up with years of the same tedium that any student who showed any spark of imagination was a treasure to be encouraged. Hence Beeb's high marks. Earle did, however, accuse Beeb of being "gratuitously eccentric in his arguments".

Beeb shrugged and smiled in response. He replied, "If you structure your argument well enough, and present your case with enough style, you can convince almost anyone that you've proved almost anything."

Earle nodded in agreement, and I suspect wondered to himself, or perhaps worried, that young Bowmore might pursue a career in politics.

For the next two years our class dominated the results in English for the school.

I think that the unconventionality of our teacher and most of our best and brightest irked the Head of Department. Mister G. C. Carter, more usually known as 'Magna', presented himself as a progressive and edgy educator. In some ways I suppose he was. Selecting *Siddhartha* for the curriculum was evidence of that. But I reckon it was a pose. A façade to disguise an underlying conservatism – and when he reviewed some of the work that Earle's pupils were producing it made him uncomfortably aware of how shallow his pretensions of being avant-garde really were. Charitably, perhaps we were doing what he'd really wanted but had been restrained from by circumstance and position. Whatever its origin, there certainly seemed to be a measure of resentment.

That helped to bond us over those two years – pupils and teacher. There's nothing like a common enemy to forge an alliance. It didn't go unnoticed. Early in the first term of Grade 12 I'd made it to the top of our class with a fervently Scottish nationalist deconstruction of *Macbeth* as political polemic that completely rewrote history just to further Shakespeare's own mercenary requirements. It sat well with Earle's own Welsh patriotism, and during our group discussions the sentiment caught on. Virtually everyone's assignments took one or other side of a nationalistic agenda, Scottish or English.

Magna Carter's response was to determine that our second term syllabus was entirely composed of Irish writers. Joyce's *Portrait Of The Artist As A Young Man*. Synge's *Playboy Of The Western World*. The poems of William Butler Yeats. Oscar Wilde. Shaw. Congreve. Goldsmith.

Our response, after slogging through the required reading, was to discuss and compare our set writers with other offspring of Erin we considered more interesting. People like Bram Stoker, C. S. Lewis, Samuel Beckett and of course Spike Milligan. It was an effective way of getting us over an immediate negative reaction to Irish literature in general, and full credit to Earle for devising it.

The end of our final year of school was marked by the awarding of School Prizes for the 'best' student in each subject. You might think this would be determined by overall academic success – a simple equation of who had the best marks. But to overcome any discrepancies between the generous or otherwise assessments of different teachers, the Prizes were determined at the discretion of the Heads of Department.

We were disappointed but hardly surprised when the English Prize went to the star pupil of a different class. His marks had been at or about those of Beeb, me, and another of Earle's cohort, but he was captain of Magna's champion school debating team, and wrote detailed and well-researched essays. Not especially creative, but conventional and by Carter's lights 'suitable' literary criticism. It was expected that the boy would go on join the ranks of past pupils to have a successful career in conservative politics – just the sort of alumni the school treasured. Nearly as much as sportsmen who represented their country.

Earle expressed his sympathies at our final English class/group discussion. I admit to carrying a bit of resentment, fatalistic as I'd been about my prospects. Such a sentiment didn't seem to afflict Beeb, though. He was more consoling of me, and indeed Earle.

"I'm sorry you didn't get the recognition you deserved, sir," he quietly told the teacher as we left his classroom for the final time. "For what it's worth, you've given me a lot of entertainment as well as education for the last two years. And you've really helped me appreciate our language. Thank you."

The two shook hands. Seccombe was moved, as you might expect.

I could see it in his eyes when I took my turn to shake his hand and echo Beeb's sentiments.

"It's been fun – thanks, sir. I've enjoyed it, and gotten a lot out of it," I said.

I didn't say it, perhaps didn't really realise it at the time, but one of the most important things I got out of that English class was an enduring friendship. You don't get so many of them in your life that they're readily forgotten.

2

BIOLOGY

Not all of the teaching staff shared Earle's appreciation of Beeb's agile mind. Throughout Grade 11 Beeb was the bane of Jim Gladstone's life. Jim taught Biological Sciences. This subject was an untidy amalgam of zoology, botany, physiology and basic sex education.

It might be this latter component that explained why it was the one science subject to hold much appreciation among those of us who'd elected to pursue a Humanities stream during our final two years of school. Grades 11 and 12 presented our only opportunity to exercise any say in our own academic destiny, picking two-thirds of the six subjects we would study in those years. A one-off, no turning back, choice had to be made at the end of Year 10. Two subjects were compulsory for everyone: English and Basic Mathematics. Four other subjects were required. No practical options like Technical Drawing, unfortunately – not Academic enough for our school. I never understood why architects weren't regarded as 'professionals' in the same way as accountants and teachers. A long-standing historical bias, I suspect. The menu of choices fell into two categories: Science and Humanities.

I don't know that the term 'Humanities' gets used much anymore.

For the sake of clarity, I'll explain that it was a catch-all that referred to History (Ancient and Modern), Geography, Economics, Music and Languages (German, French or Japanese – only one of which could be chosen). What the subjects all had in common was that they weren't taught in a laboratory. As for the collective name, it was never explained. We applied our own interpretation: science was intrinsically inhuman.

All too many of my peers made their choice of subjects based on the career path already laid out for them by zealous parents and Guidance Counsellors. Physics, Chemistry and Advanced Mathematics for those Fate (or someone else) decreed destined to be in some branch of the medical profession. Or in a research lab splitting atoms, constructing polymers or mutating fruit flies. Advanced Maths and Economics for the accountants-to-be, and often for the lawyers-to-be. Language, Modern History, Geography and Economics for those intended for diplomatic service.

It struck me as sad then, as it still does now, that so few of our number seemed to select subjects that they actually liked and were interested in, instead of what was expected of them. For all that Beeb and I had plenty of pressure from our parents to Do Well, at least we were in the fortunate number who didn't have our lives already planned for us. The other side of that coin would be to consider us rudderless, but we were okay with that. Destiny would find us without our going looking for it. Direction was a matter of option, not obligation.

Biological Sciences was an option we both chose, not (just) because of the sex education element, but because we both had thought that if a bloke was going to understand Life at all, it would surely help to know something of how it actually worked. In hindsight, a lot to ask of a Secondary education, even at a school like ours. We didn't know how much we didn't know, and alas, neither did many of the teaching staff.

The Head of the Biol. Department, Joe King (yes, as in "You must be…" – no nickname required there) cannily put all of the Humanities stream pupils into one class. Joe was very much a Science man himself, but he had a surprising affinity for music and poetry. As much as he didn't want his classes of serious science students distracted (or diluted, perhaps) he also thought that artistic temperaments would be better served by mutual support.

The extremely intelligent but otherwise hapless Jim Gladstone was one of a breed already becoming scarce by then - a Creationist science teacher working outside the church school system.

He was sincere and earnest in his beliefs, and spent considerable time in and out of class debating them with several strongly opinionated students. Most of them argued from positions of their own dogma or belief systems, point to counterpoint. "Darwin says..." versus "Scripture says...".

Beeb didn't hold fast to any such firm contra position. He didn't argue *for* any particular belief or philosophy, he just refused to simply accept what he was told.

Faith was persistently challenged by rationalism and requests for evidence. Beeb would pursue curly questions and lead Jim down sidetracks far removed from the curriculum. Jim's own enquiring scientific mind didn't help. He wasn't about to change his fundamental dearly-held beliefs, but his intellectual curiosity was readily piqued. He'd research and discuss papers that Beeb had turned up, and points his perplexing pupil put to him.

The curriculum was all too often forgotten or glossed over. It was probably a small miracle that anyone in our class actually passed Biological Sciences in Grade 11.

When we came to our final school year and changed teachers, Beeb found himself in a Biological Sciences class taken by a man who was Jim Gladstone's polar opposite.

Frank Simonson was primarily on the teaching staff because he had been a world-class rugby union player who had attended the school as a boy. They were probably the two biggest assets a bloke could have on his Curriculum Vitae when seeking a job in our institution. Appointing a full-time rugby coach was not the Done Thing in those days, even in the Teflon-coated elitist environment of Greater

Public Schools. The school's academic excellence was still of primary importance, nominally at least.

To accommodate that nominal priority, while still doing everything possible to win a cabinet-full of sports trophies and championships each year, sports coaches had to be seen to offer some credibility as educators. The teaching ranks included State and international cricketers, ex-Wallabies, and sundry Olympians who at least held an undergraduate degree and a Diploma In Education.

The heroes of the playing fields were slotted into teaching posts where it was hoped that they could do little damage. The staff common room did host plenty of highly qualified teachers – Masters of Arts or Science, Ph. D.s even - who would nurture the good, interested students who had real academic potential. And to be fair, none of the coaches-who-taught were dills. Frank had, after all, managed to complete a science degree during his University rugby career.

Frank Simonson wasn't stupid, but neither was he subtle. He approached teaching as he had approached opposition defences - head on, direct, no sidestepping, straight out of the playbook. Sex education classes with Frank were sometimes like readings from the Letters page of Penthouse magazine, and other times like reading the instruction sheet for a make-it-yourself bookcase ("Insert tab A into slot B..."). Romance wasn't a consideration, and passion was reserved for the football field.

The bull in a china shop approach had served the former front-rower quite satisfactorily in his new academic career. That is, until he encountered Beeb.

Frank made it clear to the class early in the year that as far as he was concerned evolution was a fact, not a theory, and he would teach accordingly.

Another teacher later confided to me that one reason Frank had taken this adamant stance was just to annoy Jim Gladstone. Simonson reportedly regarded Jim as a "bloody drip who wouldn't recognise a rugby football if you bounced it off his head". Frank apparently knew this from experience as they'd been at school together and he'd tried it more than once.

After the debates and sidetracks of the previous year the class probably thought we might settle down to relative peace and quiet, and something like the prescribed curriculum.

It didn't work out that way. Beeb took the theory of evolution and picked at it. He picked all around it and picked it to pieces. He challenged Frank's evidence and reasoning with even more relish than he'd shown fencing with Jim Gladstone's religious beliefs. And again, we started spending class time 'off topic', disappearing down academic rabbit holes.

Simonson didn't have the intellectual nous of Jim Gladstone, but if a student was going to disagree with him about evolution, by God he'd make a fight of it as best he could. Even he knew that "Because the syllabus says so," was an inadequate answer that made him look weak.

Outside the classroom one morning, after one of the more particularly intense discussions about the origins of life I accused Beeb of deliberate bloody-mindedness. "You're arguing for the sake of it!" I said.

"Not at all," he replied. "Just because I disagree with one doesn't automatically mean I have to agree with the other. They may well both be wrong, after all. Life on Earth may have started in some quite unexpected way that nobody's considered yet." Eric von Daniken's books were achieving paperback notoriety around then. *Chariots Of The Gods* was blurring the lines between speculation and science. Our conversation headed off on some fanciful tangents from there.

Back in Frank Simonson's Biological Sciences class days later Beeb was much less light-hearted.

"But sir," he protested, "there are demonstrably huge gaps in the so-called 'fossil record'. There isn't just one missing link in human evolution, or equine evolution for example, far less between species – there are whole chains-full missing. It's like joining the dots, and leaping straight from seventeen to fifty-four. You might get a picture, and quite possibly the one you want, but that doesn't mean it's right."

Even Frank's limited imagination got that particular simile. Got it, but didn't like it. He changed tack, and drew on another chapter of our textbook that referred to demonstrated similarities in DNA structure. His contrary pupil listened politely, intently even, then shook his head and once more put his hand up to be heard.

"Sir, such genetic 'evidence' as you've put forward is subjective. It's equally open to some very different interpretations. Just because there are similarities between my DNA and that of a white mouse, it doesn't mean we both came out of the same hole in the wall. We're both carbon-based life forms, made of the same fundamental raw materials, so surely it makes sense that there's a resemblance at a cellular level."

"Well of course, boy. That's what I've been saying…"

"But resemblance needn't imply evolution. Sir, a slingshot and a jagged rock are made up of the same fundamental raw materials as the cathedral at Notre Dame, but other than their mutual connection with stories of Israel's King David could you really make a case for one construct being the 'evolutionary base' for the other?"

The teacher's eyes narrowed in thought as he tried to remember who King David was. No matter, he understood slingshots and cathedrals.

"They're both made of stone and wood. There's just a big gap in complexity between them. Like there is between a single-celled amoeba and a bloody-minded schoolboy."

That got a laugh from the whole class, Beeb included, but it didn't deter my mate from continuing.

"Quite right, sir – I agree. But does that mean that we can draw an evolutionary line to chart that complexity? At what point did the idea of a slingshot become a house, which became a church and ultimately a cathedral? Couldn't those things have been conceived, designed and built independently of each other?"

It was a question that provoked input from other students. We were a group of Humanities scholars, after all. Yet again the reins slipped from Frank's grasp, and that particular Biological Science class turned into a group discussion of the history of architecture.

For a few weeks our attentions shifted from the philosophical to the purely practical as we examined the mechanics of anatomy and physiology. That brought its own challenges and distractions but at least didn't present the same opportunities for Beeb or anyone else to delve into cosmic awareness.

But before Grade 12 was over we'd returned to the matter of the nature of matter. Our analysis of cell structure inevitably led to questions about how such structures had come about.

It seemed innocuous enough when Beeb asked, in relation to a particularly complex arrangement of cells, "Where did that come from, sir?"

The reply pointed to a simpler but similar arrangement.

"And where did *that* come from, sir?"

It only took a few repetitions of that question-and-answer cycle to move us from the demonstrable to the theoretical, and of course the Big Question of where and how it all started. Frank stuck firmly to the non-Creationist syllabus line that led through Darwin and beyond to a distant point in a primordial universe.

All that got from Beeb was a look of puzzlement. "But sir..." he said (a phrase that Frank had come to dread hearing) "But sir, to accept without question a hypothetical process of evolution from a supposed cosmic 'big bang' of unknown origin is as much an exercise in faith as accepting Mr. Gladstone's creation in seven days by an unfathomable God. All it does is to substitute the word 'science' into the position of Supreme Deity."

"But bloody Glad- er, *Mister* Gladstone says you don't agree with *him*, either."

In desperation, Frank had resorted to discussing his vexatious Grade 12 pupil with his long-time rival, hoping for clues to counter the stubborn arguments.

Beeb only shrugged at Simonson's frustrated comment. "Not especially, no, sir. I don't think the answer has to necessarily be just one thing or the other."

The science teacher sat heavily in his chair. "Well, Bowmore," he sighed, "Dare I ask, what are *your* thoughts on the origin of the species?"

Beeb looked at him mildly and said "Sir, I'm not remotely interested in the origin of our species. I wasn't around when it happened. I'm more concerned about the future of our species. I've no wish to be around for the end of it."

The class full of Humanities students erupted in discussion about human-led environmental change, pollution, the degradation of water and forests, changes in disease immunity and antibiotic resistance. Things that were getting increasing media coverage, even in our notoriously conservative newspapers. They weren't often mentioned in the sports pages, though, so hadn't been high on our teacher's list of Matters Of Concern.

While the Queensland High School Science syllabus apparently gave little guidance on alternative theories of the origins of the universe, it seems to have been completely silent on the management of teenage social conscience. Frank blinked. He was as out of his depth as a laboratory mouse thrown into an Olympic swimming pool.

While he'd lost control of the discussion, he could at least be a spectator as different pupils took different positions, frequently reflecting their own parents' place in industry or business. The son of a sawmill owner, even if he habitually argued with his parents, had a different perspective to the son of a botanist. The industrial chemist's son who was studying Humanities as a reaction against a stultifying dull home life nonetheless had a different mindset to the son of two successful Creative Artists.

Beeb said little more. He was satisfied. He'd got his peers thinking, not just nodding as they absorbed dubious 'facts' to recite by rote. He didn't have to agree, or disagree, with anyone.

For Frank Simonson, the rest of the lesson time was perplexing and in a strange way exhausting. It was a massive relief when the bell rang for the end of the period. He had probably never been happier to hear its sound when he had been a student himself.

3

BUTCHERY

Our study of Biological Science wasn't just theoretical. A few times per year we got 'hands on' with Practical Classes. (Alas no, there was no version of these during the sex education component of the course.) Somewhere, somehow, someone had made the decision that the most effective way to teach anatomy was to get us to cut up dead bodies.

Not human bodies. That would have been a bridge too far even for our "leading educational institution". But we did get to work through a representative sampling of the wild kingdom.

These 'prac' classes weren't for the squeamish, but in their way, I suppose they were effective. You get a real sense of a body being "a bag of meat wrapped around a hollow tube" when you have all of the 'bits' laid out so as to expose a complete digestive tract running from one orifice to the other. I wonder how well Jim Gladstone would have dealt with this part of the curriculum. Being a thoughtful man doesn't mean he was necessarily sensitive about cutting cadavers, however clumsily. I do suspect, though, that he'd have been more respectful of the deceased critters than Frank Simonson.

For Frank, the dead bodies were a resource, nothing more nor less. If some bloody drip of a boy stuffed up a dissection, either through clumsiness or a perverse desire to test the elastic qualities of a length of intestine by flicking it like a rubber band, to see how far across the room it would fly, well, his only concern was inconvenience. Would he have to arrange for another specimen to be defrosted and prepared?

Ah yes, the preparation process. The setting up of all of our laboratory classrooms, for all branches of science, fell to one member of the school staff. Test Tube Ted, whose official title was, I think, Laboratory Manager. He was responsible for laying out, and cleaning up, all of the scientific equipment that was used: test tubes, chemicals, Bunsen burners, petri dishes, microscopes, dead bodies. The students were expected to clean up after themselves, but there was an unspoken recognition that it wouldn't always, or often, be done adequately to ensure that the equipment was ready for uncontaminated use in another class. Like washing a plate that's come out of a dishwasher with a crust of dried gravy still attached, Ted would clean up after the cleanup.

Ted was a tall, quiet man. He had a thick thatch of greying hair that belied a face that looked too young for it. I'd guess he was in his late 40s. Whatever time of the year, Ted always wore the same outfit: grey slacks, white shirt and a brown cardigan.

He didn't interact with the boys much if he could help it. Actually, I don't think he interacted with the teachers very much more. Ted was a man of few words. Those that we heard were unfailingly polite, but usually delivered in a low reluctant tone that suggested he found conversation as appealing as a cold meat pie and a warm beer – not toxic, but better to be avoided.

His domain was a small office at the far end of the Science Block, and more importantly, his storeroom. This was, for the scientifically-minded students, an Aladdin's cave. As well as the mundanities of test tubes, beakers and burners, it held chemicals, scopes micro- and tele-, and a range of intriguing electrical equipment. And a freezer full of dead critters.

Before the start of each Anatomy (Practical) class, Test Tube Ted would deposit on each long desk a quantity of metal trays (one per two boys). They were much like baking trays, ranging between four and six inches deep. There was a half-inch layer of wax on the bottom of each tray, to accommodate the pointy ends of the pins that were in a small jar that was also placed on each desk.

Each tray held water up to a level approximately half an inch above the specimen that was the most important content. These had been removed from the freezer and allowed to thaw in plenty of time for us to be able to dissect tissue that wasn't as hard as ice. Evidently all of the victims had been frozen fresh, as there was never a whiff of decay or decomposition.

Curiously, Ted's treasure-trove didn't include scalpels. We were expected to provide our own. An addition to the Required Texts list at the start of the school year that raised a few parental eyebrows, I'm sure. Not the easiest equipment to obtain, either, for parents whose 'school shopping' encompassed only a bookstore and the uniforms section of a big department store. Some, like my folks, talked their regular GP into parting with a scalpel and an assortment of blades. Beeb's enthusiastically creative mother was able to acquire the necessary implement via one or other of her Craft classes – apparently a scalpel could be an effective sculpting tool in sensitive hands. Unlike the hands of most schoolboys, as we shall explore soon.

Upon our arrival at our prac class, we'd be confronted by our jar of pins and metal dish, in which lay our victim, sorry, subject for the next few days. We started our vivisection journey on something theoretically simple – the earthworm.

Simple in the anatomical sense, that is. Helpfully light on for skeletal structure, and nothing too complex among the internal organs (although the hermaphroditic reproductive bits presented some surprises). But even a good-sized earthworm is not a large object upon which to be applying the pressure of a scalpel for the first time.

The *idea* was to slit open the skin for the length of the worm, with smaller horizontal slits top and bottom, like a serif capital letter I. Then we could delicately fold the skin back and pin it to the wax to reveal the internal structures, all suspended in the water for ease of study.

The reality was that more than half of our first batch of worms were not dissected, but bisected. Heavy-handedness saw lots of the annelids carved, slashed or hacked into pieces, only the tidiest of which fell into two neat halves divided on a central axis.

Even when the results weren't totally catastrophic for the corpse, in many cases an errant blade would cut through a major blood vessel, and the red clouds which filled the water made it impossible to see the organs that we were supposed to be examining.

Neither Beeb nor I were blessed with a particularly light touch when it came to handling a scalpel. We were among the many who prompted Frank to send a message to Test Tube Ted. Our class wasn't the first to have these problems (and I'm sure, not the last) so Ted was already prepared. A half-dozen boys were deputized to go along to Ted's domain and bring back two trays each. The trays were ready for us, waxed and wormed, with water to be added in the laboratory classroom. Apparently, he had a whole clew* of worms on stand-by, possibly sourced from a good bait shop. (*A collective noun for worms that dates back to the eighteenth century.)

Our second attempt was better. We actually got the skin split and peeled back correctly, and were going well until I opened up an artery and the water changed colour. That could be remedied though. We carried the tray to the sink and carefully tipped out the bloodied water before refilling it.

That inspired a few others to follow suit, some of them successfully. Notable failures included Beaky, who'd failed to properly pin the specimen to the wax and thus left a pile of mutilated earthworm in the bottom of the sink; Tweeter, who inexplicably refilled the tray with hot water, softening the wax which the worm promptly sank into, beyond retrieval; and Grunt who'd never mastered the art of turning a tap on gently – the thundering cascade that hit his tray splashed water, blood, and earthworm anatomy all over him and anyone else within a circle of about six feet. Unfortunately for Grunt that included Frank Simonson.

Grunt was a farm boy whose experience with practical anatomy was greater than most of us, but as he'd cheerfully explained previously, was confined to live births, routine slaughter, and casual castration. The latter of these was the dripping Frank's suggestion as an appropriate option for Grunt. He corrected himself – it would have been ideal for Grunt's father seventeen years earlier. Our teacher was not impressed at the prospect of attending the afternoon school assembly wearing a white shirt liberally festooned with bloody worm guts.

At a safe distance from the danger zone of Grunt's clumsiness, Beeb and I joined in the general mirth (quickly silenced by Frank's angry reaction) and got on with our work. We established that I was marginally more ept with a blade than my mate, so he got to do the illustration while I did the cutting. Our collective project was to draw the dissected creature, clearly labelling the major organs. We did pretty well, actually. Beeb wasn't a great artist – some of our class produced drawings that wouldn't have been out of place in a textbook – but his work was recognizable and in proportion.

That latter was a challenge that particularly defied some of our number for this and all subsequent practical anatomy classes. I remember a sketch of a rat whose brain was appeared so disproportionately enormous it looked like a hyper-intelligent mutant master of a rodent horde straight out of a comic book. Beeb or I might have made a story out of it if it hadn't been a little too implausible even for us.

After worms we moved on to amphibians. Specifically, cane toads. There was never a question of an adequate supply of these buggers. *Bufo marinus* as it was called then (now changed to *Rhinella marina* I gather – somehow doesn't sound as good as 'boofo') was in plague proportions around Brisbane at the time. I was very happy to be playing a small part in cutting their numbers – the damnable things cause terrible damage to native species, and domestic animals too.

Their negative impact comes from two causes. One is their voracious and varied appetite. The other is their toxicity. Both the eggs and the short-tailed black tadpoles are poisonous to most species that routinely eat similar things. The adult cane toad secretes something called bufotoxin, potent enough to kill a crocodile or indeed, most other likely predators in Australia.

Doing some research on our new specimens, Beeb was intrigued to discover that an extract from the cane toads' poison was being used in Japan variously as an aphrodisiac and as a hair restorer.

"Probably better to not share that bit of information," I counselled. "Among students *or* staff."

Beeb nodded. "Especially since it's also reckoned to be hallucinogenic."

"Ah. I have heard that toad licking is a 'thing' in the States. Can't say it appeals to me. Maybe they have better looking toads," I suggested.

"It's hard to imagine them looking worse," replied Beeb, eying the unattractive specimen sprawled in our tray.

He tapped the shoulder of Test Tube Ted, who had been running a bit late and was just leaving the room as we early arrivals got to our desks.

"Excuse me Ted," said Beeb. "Are you sure we've all got toads and not any native frogs? I gather there are a few that look similar."

Some blokes might have taken affront at their competence being questioned, but not our Lab Manager. He seemed to appreciate Beeb's concern for the native wildlife.

"Check the eyes," he replied. "Our frogs have got irises that are vertical. Those toads have got ones that are horizontal slits. Like the line that gets ruled through a text that's wrong."

"Marked for deletion? Thanks – that's a good way to remember!" said Beeb.

It had been perhaps the longest speech any of us had heard Ted give. He nodded acknowledgement of Beeb's thanks and left the room without another word. His face wore a smile though, which wasn't often the case.

The toads proved easier surgical subjects than the worms. They were considerably bigger, for a start! Their dissection was attacked with rather more enthusiasm, too. None of the class had any sympathy for the species. Even Frank disliked them.

"They should never have brought the bloody things into the country," he said. "Supposed to eat cane beetles up north, but they eat every other bloody thing but! Oh well, I suppose they ate the beetles too, but not many of them. Other stuff was easier to get to."

"How so, sir?" asked Beaky.

"Cane beetles tend to live up the top end of the cane stalk." Frank jabbed a finger at the specimen in a nearby tray. "These fat buggers are lousy climbers. Rather live and feed at ground level. They'll eat any bloody thing, too, dead or alive. Lizards, mice, frogs, the eggs of anything that nests low down, even bloody crocodiles!"

Some of the class added their own observations as to what they'd seen or known cane toads to devour – pet food, a fledgling bird that had fallen from its nest, even dog turds.

"Even more omnivorous than a sheepdog, or even the average schoolboy," observed Frank.

Dissecting the upper intestinal tracts of some of our specimens gave some proof to this assertion. We found evidence of various types of plant, skinks, moths, dry cat food, cockroaches, even a recognizable fragment of a cracker biscuit.

Unfortunately, we all got a memorable insight into the fate of these food items thanks to the surgical ineptitude of Grunt Belvedere.

Grunt's study partner Tex McKenzie had determined that Grunt couldn't draw a straight line with a ruler, so he (Tex) would do the artwork for the pair and leave the scalpel in his mate's large hands.

The farmer's son had done a fair job up to a point. Tex was peering closely at the tray (in later life he'd wear serious prescription glasses) getting a sense of the arrangement of organs for his diagram. At this point Grunt chose to emulate some of the other students who were examining their toads' stomach contents. Alas, Grunt couldn't tell one part of the intestinal tract from another.

It wasn't blood that billowed out into the water. It was thicker, browner, and vastly more pungent. The smell was distressingly obvious at the far side of the classroom, but especially distressing for Tex, who'd been an inch or two away. His immediate vomit added to the appalling soup in the tray.

Showing great presence of mind, Grunt rushed to the sink to wash out the mess. Regrettably he'd learned nothing about the use of the tap from his earthworm experience. Again, the water hit the tray as a thundering cascade, and again the splash zone had a radius of a good six feet. And again, the person in the second-closest proximity after Grunt was the luckless Frank Simonson.

Class dismissed.

Fortunately, Grunt was a boarder at the school so he could be immediately directed to return to his dormitory for a shower to remove toad faeces and Tex puke broth from his face and hair. His uniform was probably irredeemable but was shoved into the boarding house laundry chute anyway, where it would contaminate the clothes of the next poor sod to innocently deposit their clothes for washing.

Frank didn't have such an on-site luxury. He headed straight for the changing rooms under the school gym, aiming for a hot shower and the rugby gear he'd intended to wear at the afternoon's training session. The aroma would linger though, and both Frank and Grunt were given a wide berth for a while.

The windows and doors of the classroom were left open, and the ceiling fans on High. Ted strung black and yellow tape across the doorway, with a large sign that read, "Keep Out! Bio-hazard!" The sign wasn't really necessary - nobody with any sense of smell would be going in there if they could help it. We didn't often think about the anonymous cleaners who plied their trade around the school every evening, but this was one occasion on which they had the sympathy of our whole class. Beeb even left a note on our behalf attached to Ted's sign. It simply said, "Sorry!"

From toads we graduated to *Mammalia*, specifically rats. These, we learned, were Test Tube Ted's least favourite specimens. They presented the most work for him. Because of the perceived health risks, every individual specimen had to be thoroughly cleaned and disinfected, both before freezing and after defrosting. I think they may have been high-temperature steam-cleaned, similarly to a dentist's equipment.

To everyone's great relief, no significant dramas befell any of our class's subject rodents, beyond an unidentified prankster's experiment with rat gut's elasticity and aerodynamic properties.

The last of our 'study materials' for Anatomy (Prac.) were surprising, and for some, a little disturbing. No one cared greatly about worms. The pest species cane toads and rats were exterminated willingly. But there were eyebrows raised when we arrived at class to find our dissection trays each bearing an eight- to ten-inch long baby shark.

The movie *Jaws* had been released a little while earlier, so for some at least there was a case to be made for "culling a dangerous predator". It wasn't much of a case though, not least because what we had weren't even Great Whites. They were yellow.

I'd thought that was a result of some sort of preserving fluid they'd been kept in, but no, it was their natural colour. A trawler (I guess) must have caught a large number of juvenile Lemon Sharks, maybe even a school. Then someone on our school's Science staff bought the entirety as a 'job lot' at the fish market. I'm pretty sure it wasn't Ted, judging by his quiet grumblings about how much freezer space they took up. I think he'd have been quite glad of some worm-style surgical incompetence so he could put out replacements, but we were a bit more adroit with our scalpels by now.

Those who cared were reassured that this species was *not* endangered, and in fact bred quite prolifically in mangrove areas not far from Brisbane. Unlike a lot of sharks, they tended to stick to just above the sea bottom, although often in waters so shallow the distinction wasn't obvious.

Not surprisingly, it was Beeb who did the research and revealed to the class that while the Lemon Shark was indeed abundant locally, that wasn't the case internationally. The species had become scarce, even non-existent, in places around Southeast Asia. It was suffering from pollution, habitat loss, and overfishing. There was a market, inexplicable to most Australian palates, for shark fin soup, and the slow-moving Lemon was an easy target. All the more appealing because it bore two dorsal fins of similar and substantial size.

Even Frank, a regular angler, was unimpressed by the 'fishing technique' of netting the sharks, hacking off the fins, then throwing the maimed creatures back into the sea to drown or be attacked by other predators. Our teacher wasn't the most sensitive bloke on the planet, but neither was he a cruel man, and this seemed an indefensible treatment of an animal.

So, these subjects for dissection were mostly treated with rather more respect than the three species that had preceded them. Not completely respectful. Shark jaws, even ones that only measured a few inches across, were an irresistible toy for some. More than one set were removed and found their unpleasant way onto unwary fingers, arms or other tender anatomy.

This wasn't a game that Beeb participated in, though. Neither as villain nor victim. He found the whole 'up close and personal' approach to physiology more interesting than he'd expected.

We talked about it over iced coffee and ham-and-salad rolls (mine without the salad, thank you) one lunchtime.

"I'm really struck by the fragility of these things called bodies," Beeb said.

"Especially under the hands of someone like Grunt Belvedere," I added.

"Well, yes, that's true. But even under ordinary circumstances, when you look at all of the component pieces that make a body, whatever species, actually *work*, and look at what holds them all together..."

"Complex, definitely. I'm not sure I'd have used the word 'fragile' though," I replied.

"Oh, I know some tissue types are tough, in their way. Bone, sinew, even intestinal walls, Grunt notwithstanding. But there's a... delicacy to the way it all fits together that fascinates me. It makes it hard for me to believe that all these various versions of life sprang into existence and evolved by some sort of happy accident. I'd probably never say that in front of Jim Gladstone, of course," he admitted with a grin.

"No. But you are right. It's a bit hard to see a single celled amoeba spontaneously generating lungs, or gills, or guts or limbs or fins. Like you said to Frank once, it's not links that are missing, it's whole chains," I agreed.

Beeb looked thoughtful, and we lapsed into contemplative silence for a few minutes before he spoke again.

"The other thing I've realised is that, while we've taken apart the mechanics of how a body works, I'm no closer to understanding why it does. What actually animates it? Us?"

"Spirit? Soul?"

"Whatever name is applied. Some *thing* that's the spark of life. I understand that there are, let's say, mechanical things that can turn that spark off – stopping the heart, cutting the head off..."

"Squashing. Suffocating. Drowning or dissecting. Various gruesome or unpleasant acts according to species," I mused.

"Yes. Or sometimes just age. Years for us, days for some insects. But what exactly is it that stops? I mean, if we were to reassemble all of those bits in one of those trays, properly, why couldn't you plop the shark back into Moreton Bay and watch it swim away? All the physical components would be in place. Just not 'life', whatever that is."

"Brain activity?"

Beeb shook his head. "That's another mechanical function, I think. Amazingly complicated, of course."

"If the human brain was simple enough to understand, humans would be too simple to understand it."

"Well said, Paddy!" he laughed.

The bell rang to summon us to an afternoon's contemplation of the decline and fall of the Roman Empire. As we tossed our bottles and paper bags into a bin Beeb gave a decisive nod.

"There's a lot I don't know, and probably never will, but these anatomy pracs have taught me one important thing.," he said.

"What's that?"

"I have absolutely no desire to become a surgeon!"

"Amen, brother, amen!"

4

____

BULLY

A remarkably far-sighted innovation that the school offered in Grades 11 and 12 was an Option class for two hours every second Friday. This was a time to pursue subjects that weren't on any formal State syllabus.

For some, it was an additional opportunity for sports, perhaps a new discipline or more intensive training in one element. Single scull rowing had a small dedicated group, rugby refereeing an even smaller following.

There were more academic options too, such as Political Science, Botany, Indonesian Language, and the one that drew both me and Beeb in: Journalism.

In part this was because the classes were run by Earle Seccombe, for whom we both had a lot of regard. Respect even, insofar as fifteen-year-olds understood it. But we were also there because we'd become interested in the English language and how best to apply it.

Very early in the piece I observed that the class had been fostered by the head of the English Department as a means of having the annual School Magazine put together without having to dedicate too many of his own resources to it.

Beeb suggested that this was a rather cynical suggestion, but then remarked, "The interesting thing about cynical insights is how often they turn out to be true."

"That's a very cynical thing to say," I replied, sharing his grin.

Under Earle's tutelage we did learn quite a lot, much of which I found useful in later life. We didn't always realise in detail what we were learning, but it was good practice in using words differently. One thing that stuck was the very early instruction: "To be a good effective journalist, you must first forget everything you know about creative writing."

There were two parts to this. It meant that content had to be factual and concise, not imaginative. It also meant that the writing style had to be pared down to minimalist – simple language, short sentences and paragraphs.

"Assume you're writing for someone under ten, gentlemen," Earle explained with a note of sadness in his voice. "Unfortunately, that's a generous estimation of the average reading age in this country."

"That explains the standard of most of our newspapers," said Beeb, not as quietly as he might have.

"Regrettably yes, Mister Bowmore. It's to hope that some of you here may go on to raise that standard in the future." The teacher looked around the fifteen faces in his class, some eager, some vacant, and sighed. "Hope, yes..."

There were negatives to that class. Overturning everything we knew and loved about creative writing didn't come easily to either of us. Beeb struggled to not lapse into exotic imagery, and I struggled to not slip in too much humour.

But what at the time seemed to me to be an even more important negative was that it meant an extra two hours per fortnight in uncomfortably close proximity to my bete noir of the time. Journalism class seemed an odd fit for Jan Ingersson, but there he was.

Ingersson was tall and as Nordic-looking as his name suggests. Blonde, blue-eyed, lean – he would have been Hitler's vision of Aryan supremacy. And he was a bully.

There were a few such characters around the school. Many of them got involved in sports, where they could demonstrate their toughness openly and be applauded for it. Ingersson didn't choose that path, though. There was probably too much chance of running into someone meaner and/or bigger than him.

Some bullies surround themselves with a coterie of hangers-on and sycophants. He wasn't that type either. He didn't bash people up for anyone's approval except his own.

No, Ingersson preferred to exercise his wide nasty streak in solitary ambush. After school he'd hang around near the entrance of a tunnel under a section of goods yard that was used to access one of the nearby railway stations. The tunnel wasn't long, but it was dark and often quiet.

It was a public thoroughfare, but seldom used by the public. Its proximity to a side gate of the school was handy for some of us, though, potentially saving ten minutes of walking time to the station, meaning an earlier train home. On days when he felt like amusing himself, Ingersson would lurk in the shadows, grab a passing boy who was smaller than him and either alone or in little company, and land several hard punches to the ribs, belly, or even face depending on his mood.

'Dobbing on' someone was a ticket for a very quick journey to social isolation, no matter the provocation. You just didn't tell on people, no matter what they did. Maybe it was a part of an 'us versus them', kids versus adults, students versus authority thing. Looking back, it seems pretty bloody stupid, but at the time it was an unwritten law that we all understood.

Even at home, bruises were hidden as much as possible, and more obvious injuries such as a bloodied nose were explained away as resulting from falls, accidents, or stuff that happened on a sports field. Having a parent come to the school to try to intercede on your behalf would be the height of embarrassment, and was to be avoided at all costs.

Furthermore, it was made clearly that any complaints about a beating at Ingersson's hands would only result in more, and more severe, thumping. He didn't have a 'gang' to impress, but he preened in the aura of fear that he encouraged.

I'd never have expected to find him in journalism class. He wasn't the sporty type, but neither was he noticeably literary-minded. Economics was his forte, if I remember rightly. But his father was a doctor of some note, much of whose renown came from his position as a regular contributor (possibly even a columnist) for a leading medical journal. It had been impressed upon the younger Ingersson that such a position equalled prestige and thus "opened doors". Opening doors was important in a young man's future, and so journalism studies were a means to an end.

By unfortunate chance, the class included half a dozen of us who had fallen victims to the bully's attention. All for the same reasons – we happened to be in the wrong place at the wrong time (i.e. taking the short cut to the station on an afternoon when Ingersson was feeling belligerent and laying in wait), and we were smaller than him.

Some kids are lucky enough to experience growth in a nice steady even curve, always being on, about, or even a little above the average for their age. Others get it over with early, getting big when young then gradually being caught up with by their peers. I was one of those awkward ones for whom growth came in fits and starts. I'd add an inch or two in height and overall size in a matter of weeks, then nothing for six months or more. It meant that for much of my school life I vacillated between being one of the shortest and one of the tallest kids in my class.

At the time of our early exploration of journalism I was in one of my comparatively short periods. By the end of Grade 12 I was back up to a bit more than average height, but at this time that was only an optimistic prospect. Ingersson was a good half-head taller than me, maybe even more. That and my "funny accent" combined to make me a victim of choice for him on several occasions.

Beeb was sympathetic, especially after one particular incident which left my nose rearranged to the extent that even today it's not straight. My parents' reaction was that it was my own fault if I couldn't get out of the way of a football. (Certainly that was plausible.)

For all of his social dislocation, Beeb was never targeted by

Ingersson. For one thing, he simply didn't frequent any of the spots where the descendent of the Vikings would hold his ambushes. He didn't catch the train home, so didn't use the tunnel, and chanced not to wander into any of the other isolated spots where Ingersson may pounce on the unwary. Perhaps more significantly, Beeb was close to Ingersson's size. Slightly less tall but broader across the shoulder and more solid than lean. My friend wasn't noted as a fighter, but at least looked as though he might be capable of giving as good as he got.

"He likes hurting people, doesn't he? You know, Paddy, it might actually do him good to feel some hurt himself."

"I know a few places where I'd like to hit him," I replied bitterly.

Beeb chuckled. "I'm sure. But that might just make matters worse. There are other ways to hurt someone. Sometimes more effectively."

I gingerly put a finger to my freshly deviated septum. "This feels like it was pretty effective."

It was a few Fridays later that Earle Seccombe was introducing us to another element of journalism: what he called the Probing Interview.

"I'm not talking about fluffy, light 'personality pieces' here lads," he explained. "I mean interviews that have depth and purpose, to inform, not just entertain. And that's the key – purpose. The journalist must know what he's trying to achieve. Maybe not the exact answer he wants, but certainly the question he wants addressed. Lose sight of that objective, and the interviewee is then in charge. They set the agenda, and they'll tell you what they want, not what you want to know."

He shared a few insights, tips and tricks with us, and then put it out to the class. "Who wants to have a go?"

A few hands went up. Beaky Bishop interviewed his best friend Worm Hughes on a holiday Worm had recently returned from. Fluffy Harper interviewed his best friend Chris Pearl about a project the latter was preparing for the school science competition.

Beeb was next. I sat up, expecting to be his interviewee, but with no idea of what he'd be asking about. Instead, he fixed his gaze on the Nordic youth on the other side of the classroom.

"Mister Ingersson, do you still beat up people who are smaller than you?" he asked evenly.

"Eh? What? Ah... er..." Confession was not something Ingersson regarded as good for the soul, it seemed. Not publicly, anyway. "Um... no!"

"So, do you now have some other means of selecting your targets? You don't like their face, or voice perhaps?"

"What? No, I don't... um..."

"Well, by stating that you don't *still* pick on those smaller than you, you make it clear that you've done so in the past. I'm just trying to establish how you now decide who it is to take your frustrations out on."

"Eh? What do you mean? What frustrations? What are you on about, Bowmore?"

"I'm just trying to explore your motivations, Mister Ingersson. What is behind your behaviour? You've admitted *what* you do, I'd like to consider *why* you do it."

By now, Ingersson had changed colour, and was opening and closing his mouth without producing any coherent words. Perhaps not ideal in an interview subject, but Beeb pressed on. Shrewdly, Earle stayed silent and watched the show.

Abruptly Beeb changed tack. He stood more casually, shoulders less squared, and took the hard edge from the tone of his voice as he asked, "Your father is well respected in the medical profession, isn't he?"

"Er, yeah."

"Excellent. I'm sure you're proud of him."

"Of course! But what...?"

"Out of curiosity, did he study medicine in Australia, or in Scandinavia?"

"Here. It was his parents who emigrated from Norway, years ago," Ingersson replied, clearly bemused by the new line of questioning, although it seemed harmless enough.

"Family history has been important in your household?"

"Well, um... yeah. I suppose so. Why...?"

"Were you named for your grandfather, by chance? Or another earlier relative?"

"Um, both of my grandfathers, actually."

Beeb smiled broadly and just stopped short of clapping his hands. "Ah! That explains it!"

"Eh? Explains what?"

"Why, even in Australia, there was no attempt to Anglicise your name to the more local 'John'. In good Norwegian tradition you bear their name – Jan, despite the fact that in this country that's much more usually a name used for a daughter."

Ingersson almost choked.

His implacable interviewer continued. "Does that drive your aggression, do you think? Are you consciously resentful of having *a girl's name*?"

Those last three words were said in a voice that embedded them in the minds of every single bloke in that classroom (teacher included), and would be repeated right across the school within days. 'Girl's name' never quite caught on as a nickname, but it certainly became a readily recognised tag for Ingersson, and one that blew apart much of the aura of fear he'd cultivated.

His immediate response was to start to push his way across the room, murder in his eyes. "I'll bloody get you, Bowmore!" he snarled.

Earle took his cue and stepped away from his desk to block the angry boy's path.

"That will do, Mister Ingersson! You do *not* make threats in my classroom! You've just scored yourself an hour's detention this afternoon."

"He bloody provoked me! That's not fair! You're not being fair!"

"Are you trying for two hours, Mister Ingersson? Because that's where arguing with me will take you."

The blonde boy slumped back down into his chair, scowling. Even big Scott Boof Macintosh in the seat beside him had the sense to move away, even as he joined in the general quiet snickering that was going around the room.

"Thank you all, gentlemen. That will do," said Earle calmly.

"Mister Bowmore, that was an effective example of an interrogative interview. Perhaps a little too much so, but effective. Mister Ingersson, thank you, you've provided an excellent example of how not to respond to that sort of questioning. Lose your temper and you lose any control of the interview you might have hoped for. And you will never, ever come out of the interview looking good. No matter what the – let's say, provocation. All of you, learn to take a deep breath and engage your brain before responding."

Mister Ingersson's response was a surly mumble and to look darkly around the room.

Earle didn't fail to notice the look.

"I'll be keeping an eye and an ear open, Mister Ingersson. If I hear so much as rumours of any further behaviour of the type you stumbled into admitting, trust me, you will find yourself on a steady and regular diet of afternoon detentions. Do I make myself clear?"

"Yes sir."

"Good. Now – to continue. Let's look at the process of writing up the interview. What to keep, and what to discard. Of course, we come back to my earlier point about knowing the purpose of the interview…"

It was an interesting afternoon.

Earle's threat of future detentions never had to be made effective. I don't reckon it was the prospect of the detentions themselves, though, that made the difference. The fear factor was gone. You might hit someone that laughs at you, but not many blows are going to do the lasting damage that derision achieves.

Beeb was right. There are more effective ways of hurting someone. Hurting their pride can work a treat.

5

BALLROOM

There are arguments for and against single-gender schools.

One most commonly put in their favour is that it reduces distractions during the hormone-charged days of puberty. I can't speak for the girls, but in my experience the only way to stop the average teenaged boy from thinking about sex would be to cut his head off. And/or other bits of him.

Of course, thinking about it is one thing. Actually doing anything about it is quite another, and maybe that's the real idea behind single-sex schools. Remove the close proximity of those objects of desire. Allow pupils to concentrate on their studies in class, not chatting up the person next to them.

The alternative view, however, is that it does more harm than good. A lot of attitudes and thought processes get formed and ingrained in those years, and emphasizing separation between genders makes them into The Other. Strange, inexplicable, incomprehensible creatures who aren't quite recognised as people at all. Certainly, they're not Like Us.

That's even more pronounced for those who grow up without siblings of the opposite sex. As annoying as I gather they are, at least it's some exposure to that other gender and how they think and act. You might not like them, but at least there's a bit of familiarity.

Parents are a different species. Mums and Dads aren't really female and male. Oh, anatomically they probably are, but that's really not somewhere most kids' minds want to go.

I suppose some blokes might have grown up especially close to a girl next door, but I don't really think that many Good Neighbours were quite *that* good.

Neither Beeb nor I had a sister. (Nor a brother, either.) Our exposure to femininity was limited to our mothers and the one female teacher in the school, unflatteringly known as Fossil. An expert in her subject apparently – that's how she got the job – she wore a lot of makeup, dressed severely, and was renowned for lacking a sense of humour. I suppose being largely on her own in that environment, except for the women in the office staff, she was permanently on the defensive.

That's a second-hand observation at best. Neither Beeb nor I ever had Fossil as a teacher, and she was spared the perils of lunchtime patrol duty.

Someone in the school hierarchy realised that this 'gender isolation' might have some limitations on how we'd all deal with the real world. After all, the aim of the institution was to produce the next generation of leaders, pillars of society, and captains of industry. At least some degree of social skill would be required. That meant knowing how to interact with the opposite sex, with some degree of politeness. Certainly, more than the 'nuts and bolts' we were taught in Biological Science.

The solution, someone thought, was ballroom dancing.

After school every Tuesday (so it didn't clash with sports practice), the seats would be cleared away from the big Assembly Hall and the young ladies from the neighbouring all-girl school were invited to join the boys in learning the intricacies of the waltz, foxtrot and Boston two-step, among other arcane mysteries.

Grade 12 boys only were required to participate, the whole exercise being designed to lead in to the School Formal. To get the required numbers, Grade II girls were also made welcome along with their slightly older colleagues. The classes ran for three months leading up to the big social occasion, and were led by a couple of professional dance instructors who'd apparently won numerous awards and competitions. By the look of them, those competitions had been at least thirty-five years earlier.

Three months might seem a long time for such an endeavour, but it was a well-considered time frame. For the first few weeks of classes, concentration was virtually non-existent. Concentration on the dancing instructions, anyway. We had girls. In our hands. To call that a novelty is to grossly underestimate just how new the experience was for many of us. Exciting, bewildering, wonderful, frightening – any combination of those and more, depending on the individual ego.

I rather think the girls took the classes in their stride more than the boys. Not that their school's standard of 'sex education' was especially better. As with our lot, much depended on the teacher. I know there was one woman who insisted on scuffing the shoes of all of the girls in her class. Too much shine would allow boys to see a reflection of up the skirt. And we were all on the lookout for just that, she warned. (It was an idea that had never occurred to me. Once I heard it, I was disappointed to discover just how well it didn't work.)

No, I think it was simply that, as I've read and heard so many times, "girls mature earlier than boys". One of those sweeping generalizations that is, generally, true.

After those initial weeks we mostly became familiar with the sensation of having a girl in our arms, and we started to pay attention to the dance instructors. A bit. For some blokes it even helped.

Once we had a basic familiarity with the steps some found new ways of amusing ourselves. There were races between couples, like the foxtrot derby - seeing who could complete a lap of the hall quickest. How fast could a progressive barn-dance progress, regardless of the tempo of the music? Who throw the highest kick in the Zorba? There were tests of strength in the jive – how long could you hold the girl suspended in mid-air while twirling around? Some of the more aggressive types could pick moments to clip the heels or otherwise trip an unfortunate victim (male or female). One or two particular bullies had a knack of kicking shins or calves when not being watched.

The repertoire of music played on the instructors' tinny cassette player was dated. The most modern tracks we heard were *Rock Around The Clock* and *Shake, Rattle and Roll*, meant to inspire us in the jive.

The range of steps that we were introduced to was carefully chosen to include a good number of 'progressive' dances. Not 'progressive' as in modern – I mean the type of dance where you're in circles or rows, regularly changing partners. The idea was to prevent too much 'closeness' between particular couples who might otherwise cling to each other exclusively all afternoon, opening up the experience of meeting as many potential (dance) partners as possible.

Whilst a good idea in principle, for the painfully shy, awkward and/or unattractive this could be traumatic. It's hard to say what was the worse of two lousy experiences. The "pick your partner" moments, for 'couples' dances like the waltz, which were like being picked for sports teams, when nobody wanted the stigma of being among the last chosen. Or those times during a progressive dance when your new temporary partner unsubtly looks anywhere but in your direction and makes it plain that touching you is as appealing as cleaning up after a sick dog.

I'll observe here that 'unattractive' is a very subjective term. I'm really talking about the kids, male and female, who found *themselves* unattractive. At an age of body shape changes, zits, general awkwardness, the physical impacts of rampaging hormones and unrelenting peer pressure, self-image is a fragile thing for many. There were plenty of cases where nature had been in some way unkind, and not all of the ones afflicted seemed perturbed. Conversely, there were some good-looking individuals who could never be convinced of their own attractiveness.

One advantage of the long lead-in time before the Formal was that the classes began in the middle of the year, when we were wearing our winter uniforms. Summer meant shapeless short sleeved shirts, often sweat-soaked by the afternoon – compulsory neckties in Brisbane heat were a bloody stupid idea. For Second Term though the boys wore white shirts with either a suit coat or a school blazer. The tie looked less silly, and the coat hid the sweat stains that could still be in evidence during an energetic dance. Most of us just looked better dressed up!

Likewise, quite a few of the girls admitted to being less self-conscious in their winter coats. Coats that disguised curves, or their absence, or as with us guys, sweat marks and other stains. At least by the end of that term we'd had a chance to get used to the sight of each other, and some at least could look beyond appearances and first impressions.

A number of couples had already been together long before the start of dance classes. For some it was a positive experience, adding a new dimension to an established relationship and allowing a type of public closeness that had previously been occasionally problematical. Many pairs, though, fell apart when one or other, or both, found exposure to a variety of (dance) partners presented too many irresistible temptations. Or perhaps just caused comparisons and reassessments of what was desirable.

Across three months of changing and choosing partners tentative relationships began to appear. There were those of the previously unattached (and some dissatisfied ex-partners) who were almost predatory. They were urgently seeking out The Right One, and willing to churn through as many possibilities as they could to find the desired combination of looks, character and prospects. Being dense is not an exclusively male prerogative. Neither is being shallow, or insensitive.

Beeb and I were among those who were more sanguine about it all. I was interested, sure, but I thought realistic about what I had to offer alongside many of my peers: not a great deal in the way of looks, money or ambition. Beeb had a different sort of detachment, as though he regarded our dance classes as a sort of social experiment, which in some ways I suppose they were. Mind you, he often seemed to have that attitude to life in general.

To his surprise though, he found himself being eagerly sought out most Tuesday afternoons. Competed for, even. Well, he wasn't bad looking. Reasonably tall but not gangly, solid but not overweight, pale but unblemished skin. Intelligent and polite, both of which mattered to the shrewder girls. And he could dance. That was a big bonus.

It gave him a great advantage over many of us, notably me. Whereas some blokes were just clumsy, a few of the big beefy footballers for instance, I suffered from what Beeb called 'terpsichorean dyslexia' – a chronic inability to keep the sequence of steps straight in my head. Timing wasn't my issue, just putting the correct foot forward at the correct moment. It wasn't that I had two left feet – I was equally maladroit trying to lead with either.

A month or so out from the Formal, while I was still enjoying the company of several different dance partners as we worked our way around the circles, I'd developed a particular fondness for one. Marie Hooker was quiet and rather shy. Sufficiently so that you had to look twice to realise that she was pretty, and not many bothered to. Long brunette hair tied in pigtails, fair skin with a few freckles, nice eyes and what used to be called cupid's-bow lips. Loved jazz and the theatre, and she thought I was funny. Appealingly so, I was delighted to find.

Marie Hooker – not an uncommon surname, but an unfortunate one around boys of an age when any double entendre is seized on and the smut factor played up large.

I'd added some height since my days as Jan Ingersson's target, and was better equipped to stand up for myself, or in this instance, someone else who I'd started to care about. I was chivalrous enough to break my hand on one particular guy who'd delighted in making wisecracks about whether Marie lived up to her name. Chivalrous enough to not embarrass her by explaining why my hand was suddenly in a cast, other than that I'd "hit it on something". Jon 'The

Fume' Hume didn't go to dance classes so she never got to see his remodelled chin.

Despite his preference for avoiding violence, Beeb had at least applauded my willingness to 'take a stand' on Marie's behalf. He conceded that it would be hard to 'return serve' on Hume – his lunar complexion was almost as repellent to girls as his undisguised crass contempt for them. I'm sure The Fume continued to make disparaging comments, but at least he didn't make them within my earshot.

With a large percentage of the available girls in dance class to choose from, several of whom were making no secret of their interest in him, it's probably not surprising that Beeb took up with someone unlikely.

I think she was the only Tamil girl in the school apart from her sister, four years younger. Christened Prithiya, I think, she was always called Priti. Sounds like 'pretty', which was quite appropriate. I could never pronounce her surname and won't even attempt to spell it. It started with an M, was perhaps fifteen letters long, and seemed to include at least half of the alphabet.

Pretty as she was, her dark skin and accent had a lot of blokes keeping their distance, though. Let's face it, most didn't even know what 'Tamil' meant. Several couldn't have found Sri Lanka on a map. Their loss. Priti was clever, full-figured, had wavy dark hair cut in a bob, and deep dark eyes.

She and Beeb made a striking combination, with very similar eyes set in totally contrasting complexions. I don't believe she'd set out to 'snare' my mate, they just enjoyed intelligent conversation with each other. They both told me that independently, and I wasn't going to argue. Nonetheless, several girls apparently resented her 'stealing him out from under their noses', which put her even more on the outer than her race already had.

There were unkind suggestions that the only reason Beeb had taken to Priti was because she was so unlike the other girls. Certainly, that would be in keeping with his usual contrariness. And possibly it did play some part in his initial interest in her. Most of the other blokes kept contact and conversation to a minimum, with varying degrees of politeness, so it was in character for him to pay her some attention.

But some mutual attraction did definitely develop. The aforementioned intelligent conversation was a big part of that – it wasn't an experience either of them enjoyed enough of in an average day. Physical interest seemed to evolve out of that. Mind before body, opposite to many of the relationships of their peers. Marie and I included, although compatible senses of humour were significant to us, too.

So, we had our 'dates' organized for the Formal. Comfortably, happily. Without the stress and anxiety others suffered: too many choices, or no options at all. I remember one bloke, Tweeter Knight, who inadvertently asked two different girls to the formal, and spent weeks living in mortal terror of violent retribution from the big brother of one of them.

Transport was no hassle either. No buses for us, nor the frightful expense of taxis. Beeb had breezed through getting his licence a few weeks earlier, and had convinced his mother to loan him her car for the evening. It was an undistinguished little beige four-cylinder Japanese sedan, but it had four wheels, an engine and a working radio – all the necessities. Delighting in his opportunity for automotive freedom, he volunteered to drive from one side of Brisbane to the other to collect each of us.

The locus of his journey was complicated by social requirements. He first had to drive across town to collect Priti (and Meet The Parents – more on that later). Then he had to head north, driving for a half-hour to get me, before turning around and going back to a place about eight blocks from Priti's so we could pick up Marie. Well, it was unthinkable that I wouldn't be there to meet the elder Hookers so they could a.) see the presentation of the corsage, and more importantly b.) see what sort of bloke their darling daughter would be on the arm of.

And didn't we look great? Well, we certainly thought so. I'd had the cast removed from my hand just in time, so it didn't spoil the line of the dark blue suit my folks hired for the occasion. Beeb's parents had sprung for the purchase of a classy black suit in the hope that it would serve him well in a corporate future. (It didn't.) And the girls – wow...

Satin was the fabric of choice that year. And a damned fine choice as far as I was concerned. I've had an enormous soft spot for the material ever since, I do admit.

Marie was clad in a sheath of pale metallic blue. She had magnificent shoulders, I suddenly discovered, because the dress left them totally uncovered. Slits to above the knee showed off the good legs that I already knew from her uniform. Probably best of all, from my point of view, was that her hair had at last been released from the two bands that had always imprisoned it, and the long wavy tresses framed her face and those beautiful bare shoulders in a way that took my breath away.

The colour of Priti's dress was harder to pin down. I could just call it 'yellow' but that's inadequate. Bright, but not quite. Too metallic to be subdued, too subtle to be dazzling. Paler than lemon, more interesting than canary. The dress had been made just for her, and it worked wonders on her figure. It didn't have the leg-revealing split of Marie's dress, but did have enough cleavage to prove she was better developed than a lot of the girls of her year.

Extremely well organized – an effort that I had little to do with other than saying, "Okay" to whichever of the three was telling me details – all of the collections and introductions and inspections were over and done in plenty of time for us to go for dinner before the Formal.

We (they) had selected a Chinese place in the Valley. It had a good reputation for both quality and value, and was just far enough from our schools to be out of the orbit of other couples who we'd really rather not encounter until we had to.

Furthermore, Chinese cuisine was still exotic for all of us. I know it's become a cliché that every country town in Australia has at least one Chinese restaurant, but at that time their clientele was still mostly Asian. Certainly, our families had only limited exposure to that style of food. In my case, absolutely none.

That became terribly obvious with my woeful attempts to master the use of chopsticks. The others had either enough experience, or enough dexterity, to feed themselves without too much culinary carnage. Not me, I'm afraid. After failing to grasp skerricks of Mongolian beef, or balance lumps of lemon chicken on my skinny bits of bamboo, I was reduced to attempting to spear some of the larger morsels. The ends of the chopsticks weren't really pointy enough to be very useful, though.

Ultimately Marie took pity on my plight. Her family had been frequenting their local Chinese restaurant for a while, and she knew how to work the mysterious utensils of the East. She kindly, and quite diplomatically, fed me – when she could stop giggling at my own efforts.

Even with the delay of my chopstick incompetence, we still got to the Formal on time, and unstained by spatters of sweet and sour sauce or any other Oriental condiment. We mingled a bit, but it was a night when cliques and packs dominated.

The footballers and rowers stuck together, to the chagrin of several of the girls they'd brought. Chagrin that wasn't helped by the flasks of various spirits that had been smuggled into the supposedly Dry event. There were klatches among the girls, too, based on shared interests or ambitions or social standing, apparently, dragging around their compliant escorts. Neither Marie nor Priti belonged to any of them, any more than Beeb and I fitted easily into any of the roving male-dominated packs.

There were other couples who, like us, didn't 'fit' – I suppose we were kind of a clique unto ourselves. Tweeter Knight who'd accidentally double-dated was among us, relieved to see that the girl with the big brother had forgotten all about his invitation and was hanging off the arm of one of the rugby players.

A number of teachers from both schools were present, supposedly acting as 'chaperones' to the whole event. They were hopelessly outnumbered and seemed largely disinterested – in the students' affairs at least. A few looked to be taking their own advantage of the opportunity for some extra-curricular activity, but for most the job seemed to have been gotten by the drawing of the short straw. Profiles were kept low, and a policy of non-intervention reigned in all but the most obvious loud or shrill outbreaks of trouble. There were very few of those.

All this clustering meant that the carefully practiced 'progressive' dances failed to garner much attention. Handing your partner on to someone else during an after-school dance class was one thing, but this night was much more important. For some it was display, for others it was more like proprietorship. Nearly all dancing was done in pairs, and there was very little variation in those pairings. Any attempts to 'change partners' were usually met with a degree of hostility, particularly in the more dominant groups. We misfits were a little more flexible, a little less possessive, although we were all still quite aware of who brought who, and who expected to be taking who home later.

There was a live band providing most of the music, with some recorded bits allowing the musos to take a few breaks. Ex-students, they used the breaks to load up on surreptitious longnecks of beer and bottles of rum, then relieve themselves of the ensuing bladder pressure. They were good, too. Two of them went on to achieve a measure of fame and fortune with other bands.

I suspect that they'd been given Instructions on the sort of music to be played in order to accommodate the range of dance steps we'd been taught. They were canny enough though to play to their audience. A few original songs but mostly covers of the last few years' pop and rock charts.

A lot of their playlist proved a pretty natural fit for our practiced choreography. The tempo of some songs required some tweaking for surprising results – foxtrotting to Queen's *I'm In Love With My Car*, and jiving to a medley of Status Quo 12-bar boogie (much fun!). I fondly remember a remarkably effective waltz rendition of Elton John's *Your Song*. And no-one had ever needed to teach many of us how to do the *Time Warp*.

It was an excellent night. Beeb drove us all home afterwards, in the reverse order to our collection just to reassure the parents waiting up for their daughters' safe return. And yes, we went straight home without any detours or delays for amorous adventuring.

I can't speak for Beeb, but Marie and I had already enjoyed our fair share of such activity earlier. We'd slipped out of the Formal a few times to find a quiet corner in which to further our blossoming adolescent romance.

There was plenty of that going on around the school. Some blokes actually made a lucrative business of 'renting out' keys to private spots like the Prefects' Room or Music Practice rooms that they'd been given access to. For the rest of us who couldn't afford such doubtful luxury, there were doorways, the back seats of cars, and dark spaces under trees that offered a degree of privacy if not much comfort.

The carnal pleasures Marie and I shared were clumsy, hesitant, enthusiastic, and mutually well-intentioned. By that I mean, we were as interested in each other's pleasure as much as our own. With my education based on Frank Simonson's classes (varying between dry and coarse depending on his mood) and limited exposure to a few sleazy porn magazines, and my girlfriend's not much better, we relied a lot on trial and error.

I fear there was a lot of error, especially on my part, but we were both willing triers. And remained so for quite a while after the Formal. Right up until the early days of our time at University, in fact, which is where we went our separate ways.

Amicably enough, but definite. Marie had matriculated into Medicine, and approached her studies with great determination. I fell into the Arts Faculty with no real ambition or sense of direction. We moved in different circles, soon making little effort to catch up. Our compatibility evaporated so rapidly it surprised both of us, as Marie became more serious while I swiftly became even less so.

Things were quite different for Beeb and Priti. There was some physicality to their relationship, although it wasn't talked about much other than to reflect, "That was fun!" They really were a good match intellectually and emotionally. Beeb was genuinely interested in something long-term and Priti made it clear that the interest was mutual.

The problem was the afore-mentioned parents. It wasn't that Beeb had made a *bad* impression on the night of the Formal. He just hadn't made a good enough impression.

Given time, Priti's father might have come around to accepting that his daughter was happy with a polite, intelligent young man who treated her with respect and love. Mrs. M. was, however, determined that the only suitor good enough would be a handsome young Tamil with money and serious prospects of more. An aspiring doctor from a Good Family was her ideal standard. A beige Datsun was not a satisfactory substitute for a gold BMW.

And it was Mrs. M. who ruled the roost. She held the reins of Priti's future. The girl would be going to University, yes, with hopes of finding a suitable young man. She would be studying economics, so that if an acceptable match had not been made by the eventual acquisition of her degree, she would be dispatched back to Sri Lanka to work in the lucrative finance industry there. There were relatives there who would Take Care Of Things.

As worldly as he considered himself to be, this was a cultural chasm that was too much for Beeb. Not just Mrs. M.'s attitude but more importantly, Priti's inability to stand up against it. Oh, she complained about it. Complained bitterly. But ultimately, she conceded defeat. She knew it was unfair and unreasonable, but the culture she'd grown up in was too deeply ingrained to be defied.

Together, she and Beeb might have bolstered each other but that potential obstacle was overcome by Mrs. M. ensuring her daughter was enrolled in a different University to her unsuitable boyfriend. Not sharing a campus greatly reduced the prospect of their spending time together. The girl could be pushed into a more desirable social circle – one with more boys of the right ethnicity, for one thing!

It hurt Beeb deeply. Was Priti his one and only true love? It sounds absurd at seventeen, and maybe we gave it all too much emphasis, him then and me now. But I do know he was never in a close relationship after that.

Beeb's eyes had always looked older than the years he'd seen, but now there was a sadness alongside the studied cynicism. He had a few girls who were friends, but not girlfriends in the popular sense. Certainly not lovers. Even the friendships tended to be fleeting.

Probably it's unfair to lay all the blame at the feet of one bigoted, elitist, interfering woman. Perhaps the fundamental character flaw was always going to come out anyway. Throughout school Beeb hadn't easily made close friends, of either gender. But by not long after leaving our venerable institution, he was even less inclined to try.

B.A.

6

BLUES

Out of school but still students, Beeb and I had both gone on to enrol in the Bachelor of Arts course at Queensland University. For Beeb it was an opportunity to explore in more detail subjects which were either dear to his heart or had piqued his considerable imagination. For me it was somewhere to spend some time while idly contemplating what to do with my future.

We were among the few alumni of our school in the Arts faculty. While a large proportion of our classmates had gone on to tertiary study, most of them were on track for lucrative careers in branches of medicine or science. Others who were to be seen doing B. A. subjects were there only because the degree was an integral part of obtaining a qualification in law.

Even though I'd found other social circles to move in, I still saw a lot of Beeb. Our friendship deepened during the first two years on campus as we learned more about the common interests we had, and discovered new ones.

It was early spring. We were sitting in the Uni Refectory - Beeb, me, and Miss Sally, a young lady who I was attempting to become more than good friends with. We were lunching on savoury croissants and coffee, as was our habit then.

The smoke from Beeb's Indian cigarette curled lazily up to the low ceiling. I'd given them up for over a week now, entirely for Miss Sally's sake. She didn't like "the smell of burning tea bags".

Entertainment this lunchtime was provided by a fat American calling himself Brown Water Johnson. Brown Water had settled in Australia because he knew he was on a good thing. Back home he was just another one of many pretty ordinary blues singers struggling to make a buck. Here he was a Blues Legend Direct From The USA, and money rolled steadily in.

Brown Water was growling his way through *Tobacco Road*. Beeb observed "Voice is alright. His guitar playing's nothing special, though. Not much more than two chord stuff. I could play that."

Miss Sally looked surprised. "I didn't know you played the guitar."

"Not brilliantly. Little better than this guy."

"He's getting paid for it," she pointed out.

"Yes, but he sings as well. And my voice is distinctly flat I'm afraid."

"It can't be that bad, surely," Miss Sally protested.

I interjected, "It is. It's like five miles of new freeway."

"Well alright," she replied with characteristic tenacity. "Why don't you sing, Paddy?"

"Because I couldn't carry a tune in a wheelbarrow," I shrugged.

Beeb looked thoughtful. "It's the blues, man. You don't have to sing really well, just sing like you mean it. Emote. You can do that."

Miss Sally had been smiling enthusiastically. Her smile broadened at Beeb's apparent support. "Go on, guys. At least give it a try."

So we gave it a try. We'd get together in the big old house Beeb rented in Hill End. On warm evenings we'd settle on the veranda until overwhelmed by mosquitos, but otherwise we'd be in the lounge room, sunk into enormous horsehair-stuffed armchairs, sheltered by the parachute suspended above us. The billowing silk looked nice, especially with coloured light bulbs behind it, but it reduced the effective ceiling height to an awkward five feet six.

Beeb would strum, and I would sing - well, 'emote', and Miss Sally would encourage us and pour cheap white wine from a flagon.

We started out by trying to cover other people's songs. This was not a good idea, as having a yardstick to measure our efforts by only made our shortcomings more glaringly apparent. Even Miss Sally's resolute support for what had, after all, been her idea, began to wilt somewhat when comparing our rendition of *It's Breaking Me Up* with Jethro Tull's original.

The solution was obvious. Write our own material. Utilise the creative talents we knew we both had. Nobody would ever be able to say, "That's not what that song should sound like!"

So now our sessions under the parachute or on the veranda were punctuated by frantic scribbling in note pads as we tried to pin sudden ideas and inspirations onto paper before they escaped. Beeb constructed simple but effective chord progressions over which I stretched the words we each wrote.

To my surprise it showed signs of working quite well. We were producing some genuinely interesting material. Miss Sally was almost smug, and it wasn't a matter of her being biased. I knew her well enough to realise that if we were playing rubbish, she would say so. Miss Sally was never shy with her opinions.

What soon became clear was that we had very different styles. My lyrics tended to be lightweight, or even at times downright absurd. One of my favourites was a song about a happy fish which ended up on a bread roll as my lunch. I called the song *Red Salmon Blues*.

Beeb on the other hand wrote about Issues. Passionately, although not without wit. "Joan Baez with an Errol Flynn moustache," I once teased. But he had a flair for imagery which I admired.

We quickly decided that we couldn't synthesize our styles. Beeb couldn't bear to have me trivialise any subject he felt committed to, while I felt unable to write 'seriously' without becoming maudlin.

As Miss Sally pointed out, though, our different styles actually worked in our favour. My lyrics on their own would have effectively turned us into a comedy act, which wasn't how we intended to be taken. Alternatively, a performance full of only Beeb's material might provoke suicide in a sensitive audience.

The song selection process was simple. Firstly, Beeb and I had to agree that we were both happy with a particular song. Then came the much sterner test - Miss Sally had to pass it as being worth listening to. A lot of songs which either or even both of us had been quite fond of ended up on the Discard pile. Steadily though we built ourselves a repertoire.

We were enjoying our sessions, sitting around drinking and being creative, but inevitably we got to the point of wanting to <u>do</u> something with this swag of material we were compiling.

Our first impulse was to go busking. One of our major concerns though, was the fear that if more than three people gathered to watch us perform then it might be considered an illegal public gathering. That could mean that both we and our audience would be arrested, knocked about and locked up. There was a lot of quite justifiable paranoia about the Queensland Police Force in those days, especially on campus.

Furthermore we thought that there was something vaguely undignified about singing on street corners, hoping passers by would throw money and not fruit at us. It seemed rather like an admission that we couldn't do any better, and in the arrogant flush of flexing our collective creative genius for the first time, that was an admission we didn't care to make.

Beeb suggested a free concert "for the people". That struck all three of us as a philosophically sound idea. Then we hit the hard wall of reality. Free concerts are only free for the people who attend them.

We struggled by on our Student Allowances and odd jobs. To hire a venue would cost money we simply didn't have.

To hold a concert in somewhere like a park required a permit, otherwise it would be one of those dreaded unauthorised public gatherings. We were advised that in order to get a permit from the State Government we'd have to arrange cleaning contractors, provide adequate toilet and first aid facilities, and comply with a bookful of fire and safety regulations. Then, if we had any money left after that lot, we had to hand it over as a fee for the permit.

The free concert idea was consigned to the "When We Make Our First Million..." basket.

It was perhaps inevitable that it would be Miss Sally who got us our Big Break. She'd made some useful contacts at the fledgling politically aware volunteer radio station which operated from the University campus.

As part of a continuing struggle to raise operating funds the station ran occasional concerts featuring as many cheap local acts as they could afford to hire. They were called 'Joint Efforts', usually considered an unofficial but unsubtle acknowledgement of the amount of marijuana passed around at the shows, especially those held in the University Refectory.

To our surprise Miss Sally convinced the concert organiser that a blues duo would be an important part of the "broad spectrum of modern music event" that he was planning.

Now we needed a name. Paddy And Beeb, or for that matter Beeb And Paddy, just didn't have the memorable ring that we were looking for.

I suggested that we dress up in German military uniforms and call ourselves 'The Prussian Blues'. I got no support for that idea, however it did at least start the others thinking. Miss Sally proposed 'The Light Blues'. Beeb and I rejected that one, believing it made us sound insubstantial and forgettable. And by no stretch of the imagination could either of us have been described as "light".

It was as I made this observation that Beeb leaned back in his cane chair, put his feet up on the veranda rail, sipped his wine, looked up at the heavens and said "Sky Blues".

It had everything. It described the music, had good environmental overtones, and was witty enough for my sense of humour. And without a preceding 'The' we just liked the sound of it.

We had just under three weeks to prepare a forty-five minute 'set'. Our biggest problem wasn't what to play, but what to leave out. Once again Miss Sally became the arbiter of our material.

Giving due consideration to the nature of student radio, we gave more time over to Beeb's politically aware numbers. We leavened that about two to one with some of my more surreal songs, and included a couple of short instrumental pieces in which I produced strangled cat noises with a harmonica.

Our attendance at lectures and tutorials, erratic at best, ceased completely as we poured our time and energy into our forthcoming debut.

Our diets took a turn for the worse too, as we replaced many of our meals with cheap flagon wine and packets of biscuits rather than spend time cooking or going out to eat. Admittedly for me that was less of a turn than a small deviation, but Beeb had always been a lover of good food, well prepared and presented. Miss Sally and I knew he was making a sacrifice.

Miss Sally retained some connection with the outside world. She went to a few tutorials, and made a point of eating some real meals. Our relationship, though, which had gradually become closer and a little more intimate, started to show signs of strain. Little wonder really, with my propensity for practicing until exhaustion and cheap white burgundy made me fall over.

Nonetheless she stuck by me, and us. I was never sure if it was out of love, loyalty, a sense of ownership (our act was her idea, after all), or a conviction that after the gig was over we'd all return to our semblances of normality.

They were three weeks which seemed to last forever and were gone before we knew it.

Suddenly it was performance night and there was no time left to chop and change and rearrange.

Miss Sally and some other friends had managed to secure a table at the edge of the Refectory where the concert was being held. A large space had been cleared in the middle of the room. This would at various times be a dance floor, crush space, wrestling arena, a place to fall down drunk or stoned, or totally empty according to the time of night and the style and quality of the act performing.

Beeb and I waited beside the stage for our cue to go on and set up.

The act we were following was a Radical Feminist Soul Singer who sounded like she had a sinus infection and a bad hangover.

"She'll make us look good," I offered.

"That's a little unkind, Paddy," Beeb replied. "Her lyrical content isn't bad, in places."

"She has the light touch of a bulldozer. She's so heavy handed she makes <u>your</u> worst rhetoric sound like *Summer Holiday*."

Beeb was silent. 'Uh-oh' I thought, 'I've offended him five minutes before we go on stage. Brilliant.'

He continued to stare at, or rather, through the Radical Feminist, and finally said "You're right, Paddy. Subtlety <u>is</u> important. I must be more conscious of that when I'm writing."

Well, at least he was still talking to me.

Bulldozer finished her performance to a round of wild indifference. After a final growl that sounded nothing like "Thank you, you're a wonderful audience," she stomped off.

Like all the other acts we'd been allocated fifteen minutes in which to 'set up'. With a guitar, one amplifier, a microphone and stand, and a bar stool for Beeb to perch on, that was about ten minutes more than we needed. We signalled to the crew that we'd make an early start.

While Beeb did his final tune-up I'd placed a plastic bottle full of bourbon and soda with two cups on top of the amp. It seemed the most appropriate drink for budding blues legends. I took a quick swig straight from the bottle and turned to the mike as the house lights dimmed.

The crowd looked at us unsure what to expect. Beeb wore a gaudy poncho and faded blue jeans, and sat with his head down over his guitar. I had a lurid paisley shirt unbuttoned over a black t-shirt, teamed with white jeans that sported embroidered mushrooms and a green fringe around the cuffs. In short, we were already out of fashion.

I didn't care. We were there to be brilliant. To be memorable. I shouted "We are Sky Blues! Good evening to youse!" Beeb hit a loud open chord and we were on our way.

To be honest I don't remember much of our performance. They say that's often true of opening nights and wedding days. The brain is too busy with being nervous and emotional to be storing much away in the conscious memory.

I remember it felt good. That Beeb's guitar never sounded crisper or cleaner. That my harmonica never wailed quite so convincingly. That my voice never seemed to soar, growl or purr so well before or since. I remember having fun with *Red Salmon Blues*, and that the crowd joined in with that fun.

Forty-five minutes later we were finished, as was much of the bourbon. We got a good round of applause.

That was it. Good. Better than a polite smattering, well short of tumultuous enthusiasm. We'd gotten laughs in the right places, people clapped when we wanted them to, and nobody threw anything at us.

It was enough for us to walk off stage feeling encouraged.

As we carried our gear off we were elbowed aside by one of the band performing after us. I looked down at him. He didn't look old enough to be in a bar.

A voice behind me said "'Scuse me, Paddy."

I stepped out of the way of a guy I vaguely recognised from one of my tutorial groups. He was a stringy bloke with a lunar complexion and no distinguishing character I'd ever noticed.

"Friend of yours?" asked Beeb.

"Can't even think of his name off hand," I admitted.

We packed away our small quantity of equipment, then joined Miss Sally and company at their table. Beeb and I basked in their enthusiasm. Miss Sally quite glowed with pride in 'her boys'. She was smiling the dazzling smile which had been one of the first things about her to catch my eye.

Clutching drinks we settled back to watch the rest of the show. The act who followed us were a punk band. Punk rock was the Next Big Thing, and these guys had obviously decided to jump on the gravy train early.

They called themselves The Vomit. They had all the musical

talent of four slop buckets. They hadn't even bothered to tune their guitars or drums, but it wouldn't have mattered given their ham fisted playing.

Beeb shook his head as he watched the efforts of the lead guitarist. "He makes me look like Eric Clapton," he sighed.

All that notwithstanding though, many of the crowd were on their feet, cramming the space in front of the stage and roaring their enthusiasm.

During a pause in the mayhem presented as music my spotty acquaintance, who had been maltreating a bass guitar, introduced The Vomit line-up. The underage, undersized vocalist was "Mister Excreta". The awful lead guitarist had named himself "Dash Defecate", and the Neanderthal type who pounded frantically on drums was just called "Scumm".

"Wiv two ems," he insisted.

The bassist introduced himself as "Mark Diarrhoea". Beeb looked at me in surprise and remarked "I wouldn't have thought that would be an easy name to forget, Paddy."

"Must have run straight out of my head."

Miss Sally hit me.

The Vomit's set ground on. The crowd grew more and more excited. Beeb and I grew more and more appalled.

The climax of the act came when Mister Excreta (I wonder if he was called 'Mister X' for short?) lived up to the band's name and let fly a projectile spew which spattered the first half-dozen rows of the mob crushed together at the front of the stage.

Beeb scowled. "That's definitely going too far."

"Why did he do that?" asked Miss Sally.

"Maybe his stomach's a music critic," suggested someone else at our table.

"It's cheaper than throwing flowers or drugs?" I offered.

And the crowd loved it. It was as though they'd just been blessed with a shower from a baptismal font, complete with consecrated chunky bits.

It was rare to find Miss Sally, Beeb and I all at a loss for words simultaneously, but that was the case as the crowd roared and The Vomit played (if that's the word) three encores. I'm fairly sure that two of them were the same song. The crowd seemed to neither notice nor care, though.

A little later the three of us sat under Beeb's parachute, sipping Irish coffee and reflecting on the night.

Beeb nodded to nobody in particular. "We have seen the future of popular music."

"And we ain't in it," I sighed.

Sky Blues never performed in public again. Beeb and I jammed together a few more times, but only for our own amusement.

I found a creative outlet in campus theatre, and spent more time at the bar of the Student Club.

Miss Sally and I broke up not long after the show. She left me to pursue a handsome blonde body-builder who she said "shared more of her interests". I confess to a small chuckle when I later learned that one of the interests they shared was handsome blonde body builders.

Beeb made the transition from writing songs to writing poetry. I noticed quite a bit of his work in various campus magazines and newspapers, and recognised amongst it some of the songs we'd practiced. And yes, he did display a more subtle touch.

We still bumped into each other in the Refectory occasionally. I'd talk him into coming to the theatre to see a show I was involved in, or he'd read me something he'd just written.

"Sky Blues wasn't going to work because what we offered wasn't what people want right now," I remarked to him with the sagacity of hindsight in the Student Club one afternoon.

Beeb nodded. "I'm glad we didn't try to change to accommodate them. I'd rather be true to myself than fashionable."

I smiled over my glass, and asked "Do you reckon our sort of music will come back 'in' again?"

Beeb looked at me and shrugged. "I don't care," he said.

∾

7

BATONS

During the mid- to late 1970s members of our local police force seemed to fall into one of three categories.

There were the good ones. Honest, fair-minded, motivated to do the job by a concern for justice and a desire to help and protect people. I write this now in the interest of fairness, because I'm sure such individuals must have existed. Unfortunately, it was to be several more years before I actually met any of them.

There were the corrupt ones, to be found at various levels. It could be the local copper who expected never to pay for a coffee or a meal, or who turned a blind eye to domestic violence if the bloke was a mate or a member of the same footy club. Further up the ranks there were those who took bribes and kickbacks from drug dealers and illegal gambling operations. That extended all the way to State Parliamentary level. I remember one Police Minister saying in an interview words to the effect: "You might reckon I'm crooked, and I might know I'm crooked, but it's up to you blokes to *prove* I'm crooked, eh? Ha ha ha." They were in the job to get as much out of it as possible, and not just as salary.

And there were the thugs. Some of them certainly were in the 'corrupt' category too, I'm sure, but there were those who didn't seem to be 'on the take'. It didn't make them better, just less dishonest. They liked being in a position of authority. Carrying a gun. Swaggering along the street, twirling a truncheon and being able to harass anyone they didn't like the look of. Jan Ingersson from my school days would have fitted in to this group well. Being allowed to hit people with impunity was a big part of why they did the job.

Number plates on Queensland vehicles were at the time adorned with the slogan 'Queensland – Sunshine State'. A popular car sticker of the time used exactly the same colours, size and lettering to declare 'Queensland – Police State'. Of course, I had one of those. My Dad reckoned I was mad, and while he actually agreed with the sentiment, pointed out that having it on the car was "asking for trouble".

"As long as it's near the number plate, not actually *on* it, it's not illegal," I pointed out.

"Aye, and d'ye think that'll make any difference tae an angry copper?" Dad replied.

I suppose in strict historical terms it wasn't a police state, i.e. "*a totalitarian state controlled by a political police force that secretly supervises the citizens' activities*" (thank you, Oxford). But we did have a state government who clung to power despite getting significantly less than a majority of the popular vote in elections, thanks to the way they'd changed 'the system'. And the police were certainly used as a weapon against open disagreement and protest. Certain government ministers and high-ranking police officers would eventually be found to be seriously corrupt, and were dismissed and charged accordingly, but that was still in the future while we were at Uni.

A potent weapon in the legislative arsenal was the 'anti-street march law'. It had always been the case that you needed a permit to stage a public protest, but now the right of appeal to a magistrate was taken away. The police had sole discretion as to the granting of such a permit, and it was very clear that it was *not* going to happen.

The state Premier had very publicly declared that "the day of the political street march is over – don't bother applying for a permit, you won't get one. That's Government policy now".

Have you ever noticed, or felt, the natural reaction to a "Do Not

Walk On The Grass" sign? Or one that says "Wet Paint"? Banning
street marches was never going to accomplish anything but a rise in
the numbers of people ready and willing to make their protests as
public as possible.

Not surprisingly, Queensland Uni was a focal point for a lot of the
protesting. We were being trained to think, often about Issues, and in
many cases didn't like where the thinking led us.

The dangers of nuclear energy – the risk of catastrophic accident,
and the potential for waste material to be 'weaponised' – were at the
forefront of a lot of minds. The mining and export of uranium from
Queensland, without even a show of contractual responsibility for
the use to which it would be put, was the subject of great concern. It
wasn't a lot of potentially dangerous material by world standards, but
it was significant, and the thinking was, 'someone has to make a
stand, and encourage others to follow suit'. It was a local face of a
global issue.

Street marches opposing involvement in the Vietnam War had
proved successful some years earlier – at least, they were credited
with encouraging the end of conscription. That gave them some credibility as a primary means of protesting against uranium exports. Of
course, there were no permits granted by the police. Marches
happened anyway, and confrontation ensued.

Very quickly, the *raison d'etre* for protest marches became not just
the campaign against nuclear energy, but the campaign against the
anti-march restrictions themselves. Protesting for the right to protest.
Well, that was inevitable, really. Cynics suggested that was the
government's intention all along, to be able to point to the "rowdy
illegal street marchers" and demonstrate their "law and order creden-
tials" by cracking down on such disturbances. Much easier than
cracking down on real crime, especially crime that offered kickbacks
to people in the right places.

Beeb and I were hardly immune to the prevailing mood on
campus. Neither of us could be classed as 'leading activists', but we
were both willing to speak our piece in classes, tutorials and public

meetings. And we were both willing to take our places amongst the marchers out on the streets.

Over the course of a couple of years, about two thousand arrests were made at various protests. Beeb was amongst them, though remarkably, I never was. More luck than good judgement, and I had my own run-in with the local constabulary, as it turned out.

I'd not long moved into a group house on the fringe of the CBD with a handful of other students – a couple of musos and theatrical types, a lot of fun but not a great place for concentrating on study. Of course, I didn't.

One of the girls in the household – Poolroom Jane – had taken a part-time job with Telecom as a switchboard operator at the main exchange in town, next door to the GPO. Such jobs would disappear in a few years as technology advanced and the telephone system became completely automated, but for now, there was a role for women (almost but not quite exclusively) to sit, wearing their head-sets, in front of a big panel full of jack plugs and sockets.

The money wasn't bad, not least because of the shifts involved. The switchboard operated 24/7, and there always had to be a good complement of staff on hand. A bit of earlier Union activism had seen a policy introduced that if staff finished work after midnight and before 5:00a.m., then Telecom were obliged to provide transport home, usually a taxi voucher. Of course, very few shifts then actually finished in those hours – it only happened if someone was required to work extra hours because of sickness or unavailability.

Jane was working a shift which finished *at*, not *after* midnight, so she was responsible for getting herself home. The journey from the telephone exchange to our group house was too short for most cab drivers to bother with, even among the few who were working at that hour on a week night. The distance was short enough to be walked, anyway, but there were a few dark stretches that might spell trouble for a pretty nineteen-year-old wandering alone in the night.

So, by mutual agreement, whenever Jane worked the midnight shift, someone from the household always waited outside the telephone exchange and walked home with her. Usually it was me – she was my girlfriend after all, even if we didn't share a room (a bed sometimes, but not a room) – but often one or more of the others would accompany me.

One particular swelteringly hot summer evening, while Jane was working I'd caught up with Beeb at a quirky little coffee lounge we were both fond of. We'd sat drinking jasmine tea and smoking Sobranje's for a few hours while we discussed good books we'd recently read, and music we'd been listening to. A relaxed, mellow evening, after which Beeb had dropped me home to spare me the additional walk.

The chilled, laid-back tone of the night had been such that I didn't even feel inclined to join any of my housemates in a beer when I got back. I simply lay on my bed listening to an Oscar Peterson LP and wishing we had air-conditioning. It was only when Owen tapped on my door and asked if I was going to meet Jane that I realised the time.

"Oops!" said it mildly. I didn't even bother to throw a shirt on – it was too bloody hot anyway. Boardshorts and thongs were all I needed. Owen and Mick had been up chatting over a few tinnies, and decided to accompany me.

"We'll have to get a move on, sorry," I said as I rushed out the front door.

"No worries," Owen replied as he and Mick loped after me, still clutching their cans.

We'd made it through the park in good time and were heading down Edward Street. Acutely conscious of the time, I was trotting a bit ahead of my two mates. A 'Don't Walk' light confronted me at the intersection of Adelaide Street, but I looked up to check that there was a red light to stop any traffic on that particular thoroughfare before jogging across it.

I had to break into an alarmed sprint when a white sedan came belting down Adelaide Street and ran the red light. Over my shoulder I called, "Red light, idiot!" and continued along the footpath.

Suddenly there was a squeal of tyres behind me. As the following

Mick later described it, "the bloody thing did a screechin' u-turn an' mounted the bloody footpath behind ya!"

I hadn't even looked around when I heard car doors fly open, someone grabbed me, and threw me into the wall of a jeweller's store. I suppose I'm lucky I hit the stonework and didn't go through one of the plate glass windows. Exactly what happened next is still a blur, but I know I got thrown into the back seat of the car, a large unpleasant bloke on either side of me landing punches to my ribs.

It was an unmarked police car. The only uniform was on the driver, who looked resolutely ahead while the two plain-clothes-men in the back held me pinned. The older bloke in the front passenger seat turned around. I remember his smile as he backhanded me across the face, the large ring on his finger opening up a gash from just in front of my ear. I've still got the scar.

Mick and Owen watched open-mouthed as the sedan sped away with me on board, only just remembering in time to go and meet Jane. Owen had spotted the uniformed driver, so they had some inkling of who, if not what, had happened. But none of the three of them had any clue of what to do next. They walked back to the house, fretting and tossing around desperate and unrealistic ideas.

It didn't seem clever for Jane to ring police headquarters and say, "Help! A policeman just abducted my boyfriend!" So they sat around for a while, and eventually all drifted off to bed, waiting to hear something, from someone. Nobody slept well.

My night was no more restful. After a few spins around Brisbane's streets, and a few more whacks where bruises weren't obvious, I was taken to the watch-house, where I was deposited in a cell. It was evidently a quiet night. There were only two or three other occupants, all of whom were asleep, or possibly passed out drunk or stoned.

A slightly apologetic desk officer holding a clipboard talked to me through the bars.

"What's the charge going to be?" It was like a waiter taking an order from a menu.

"Pardon? You're asking me?"

"Public drunkenness, or obscene language?" he asked patiently.

"How about neither? I haven't had a drink all night (which was unusually and coincidentally true) and I didn't swear. All I said was, "Red light, idiot" as the car went past me."

A voice came from along the hall, out of my view. "I distinctly heard the c**t swear, didn't you, sergeant?"

"Too f***ing right, Detective Inspector," came the reply from another unseen figure.

The bloke with the clipboard shrugged. I realised that he was in no position to argue. The D.I. had been named, and I recognised him as a man with a high profile as a Defender of Law and Order, apologist for the state government, and very vocal critic of anyone and anything to do with the University. I suspected he hadn't been able to get in there as a student.

I sighed. "What are my options?" I asked.

Constable Clipboard repeated the two possible charges, and told me the fines for each.

"I'm not exactly in a position to pull my wallet out," I pointed out. My thongs had been removed at the front desk, and there was nothing in the frayed pocket of my old boardshorts.

"Oh, you'll be given seven days to pay," he replied helpfully.

And so, I chose to be written up as 'drunk in a public place'. Ironic, given the number of times that I had been, without incident.

"Can I fight this in court?" I asked, when I was satisfied that the 'arresting officers' had left the building.

The desk officer shrugged. "You do have that right," he said, in a voice that made clear his advice to the contrary.

I pondered. My word, against four coppers, one of whom was a known favourite of both the government and the local media. Even if I could produce a string of witnesses to testify I'd drunk nothing stronger than jasmine tea all day, I'd have less chance than a suit of cardboard armour in a jousting contest.

I was allowed one phone call from the watch-house, but I wasn't given that option until six o'clock in the morning. Naturally, I rang the house. Naturally, it was Poolroom Jane who answered. I was too damn exhausted to be anything but calm, and managed to stem her torrent of agitated questions.

"Just bring me a t-shirt please, sweetheart," I said. "It's cold in here."

Which it was, despite it still being humid and warm outside. I guess that's why such places are called 'coolers', as well as their function in cooling off aggressive felons. Jane arrived very soon after, with the requested shirt and my wallet. I paid the fine there and then, and walked free.

"You might have at least let him wash the blood off his face!" Jane admonished the young man at the desk. The shift had changed during my stay, and this taciturn individual just grunted in response.

"No taps in the holding cells. Maybe they're worried a prisoner might try to drown themselves," I wearily suggested.

Another grunt from behind the desk. We walked out. One of the guys in the household had loaned Jane his car, so we didn't have to trudge back up the hill to home. I think I fell asleep in her arms, in whose bedroom I can't recall.

There was much outrage and expressions of support among my friends when the incident was related. Some of the folks in the house were adamant that I should have fought the charge. Beeb expressed a similar view when I told him a day or two later.

"I could vouch for your not drinking, for a few hours at least. I'm sure others could back that up. This sort of thing should be called to account," he said.

I explained my doubts about prevailing against the Detective Inspector. I'd had a further thought, too.

"Even in the unlikely event that I did get the charge dropped, and managed to stir up a bit of publicity, what do you reckon would happen? How often do you reckon our house would be getting visited by patrolling coppers? I know there's usually a stash of weed lying around somewhere. No one there needs a drugs conviction to their name."

Possession of marijuana was still a Major crime. Penalties were steep, and conviction could seriously stuff up career prospects in many professions, including those aspired to by some of our household.

"Hmm. I take your point. Even if you won, you'd lose."

"Afraid so," I said.

On the back of that experience, Beeb laid a concerned hand on my shoulder the next time there was a street march planned. He was concerned that I might already have a 'profile' that would draw more trouble for me. But I shook my head.

"The right to public assembly matters, old buddy," I said. "Matters enough to me for me to be part of a demonstration about it. I'll take my chances."

The budgerigar is a small, fragile bird. Its only defence is in numbers. It the wild, it flies in a flock so large that predators struggle to pick off an individual bird. Some get caught, but most survive. I was prepared to adopt that strategy, and be one of the flock marching down Queen Street.

It worked. That particular march ended in confrontation with the police, as usual, and as usual several protestors were forcibly removed and thrown into paddy wagons with unnecessary force. We weren't amongst them though.

A month or two later there was another march. There had been a Federal government decision to cut the education budget, again, which seemed likely to mean a reduction in the already meagre Tertiary Education allowance. That provoked its own protest campaign, distinct from the campaign for civil liberties and the campaign for safe energy – each cause having a slightly different crowd of regulars, believe it or not, although there was plenty of commonality among the faces.

Beeb and I were both among the common faces. The 'safe energy' campaign was a little dearer to both our hearts, even after my run-in with the police. Civil liberties were important, but there was a sense of it being an issue that would pass with a change of government – a nuclear disaster had global implications that transcended local politics, we thought. The Tertiary Allowance though, was our bread and butter – literally – and it needed defending.

So, we marched, and did so near the front of the crowd, if not quite in the front rank.

I think it was on Coronation Drive where things got ugly. This was a bit of a change, as much of the Trouble usually occurred in the city itself. Maybe someone senior in the Police Force, on their own or at the prompting of someone in government, thought for some reason it would be better to stage the inevitable confrontation outside the central business district. Perhaps they thought there'd be less cameras. They were wrong.

The idea, I presume, was for the police line to block the road so the march could progress no further. That was the usual strategy. What was different this time? I'm not sure. Maybe different police personnel, in charge or in the front lines. Maybe it was the change of locale – a greater sense of space, or of less 'impartial' witnesses.

This time though, it seemed like that among the front ranks of the police cordon, there was a higher percentage than usual of that 'thug' element I described earlier. Or maybe they were under less restraint for some reason. Like I said, I wasn't at the very front of the march, so didn't see exactly what happened, but from what I could make out, the not-so-thin blue line didn't wait for the lead protesters to get face to face with them, as usually happened. I think someone in uniform took it into his head to lead a charge, shield up and baton swinging.

After that, it's a blur. People on the ground, being tripped over and trodden on, a few police among the demonstrators. Headlocks and hammerlocks as people were dragged and thrown into paddy wagons. I vividly remember one guy with dark frizzy hair and a beard, curled on the ground in the foetal position being kicked by three coppers until the press of other bodies' movement took them away from him. Police batons came at us from the side as well as the front somehow. I lost sight of Beeb for a few moments, thought he must be among those 'apprehended' and hauled off, but then saw him on one knee, clutching his shoulder with blood streaming from above his ear.

Somehow I got to him, got under his good arm and helped him to his feet. We weaved our way through the melee to the back of the crowd, already dissipating into side streets or whatever other places of relative safety could be found.

The Police Minister, or perhaps the Commissioner, or both, claimed it as a "victory" because the march had been kept out of the city. They were wrong, though. The more open spaces had allowed the cameras of the press a much better view than they'd had before of what actually was happening inside the riot, not just at the fringes. There was harrowing film footage of one girl, clearly terrified, being struck on the head, from behind, by a baton.

Public opinion started to turn. Suddenly the police weren't just "doing their job", and the term "police brutality" got bandied about more than just on campus. That particular girl became a brief, reluctant celebrity, made 'the brave face of the protest movement'. She never wanted that, and as quickly as possible shunned the attention and tried to return to her studies. Despite the prompting of friends and public figures, she never pressed charges, determined that she wanted no more publicity.

I got that.

After getting Beeb to a doctor and patched up – scalp laceration, no skull damage, but a fracture to the collar bone – we watched the ensuing media circus about the girl who'd been hit.

"If what happened to you had been caught on camera, would you be willing to make a fight of it?" I asked.

"Good question," he replied after a long musing. "I suspect there wouldn't be the quite the same outrage if it was me on the footage. I think a lot of the public reaction we're seeing is because the victim is female, and even normally conservative viewers are thinking 'hang on, that's not fair', or that it's somehow crossing a line. And, she was hit from behind. At least I saw it coming and managed to duck, slightly."

"Is that really the point?"

"No, but I reckon it would make a lot of difference in court. She could legitimately argue she was trying to get out of the situation when she was hit. She had her back to the policeman. They'd argue I was 'confronting' my bloke."

That made sense. Depressing, but sensible. There was also the question of what can of worms would be opened regarding future harassment. Beeb was never part of a share house, so didn't have to consider anyone's situation but his own, but the other side of that coin was that he had no support, no witnesses to even try to corroborate his side of whatever story might be told.

"No, my friend," he said sadly. "All we can do is wait. For the wheels to turn, for some sort of justice to eventually prevail, and for the wounds to heal."

He was right, to a point. Things did change. In time, legislation improved. Some of the most corrupt individuals were prosecuted, even punished. Not all, but maybe some of those others faced trials with their own conscience, or on another plane if their 'faith' was as true as they proclaimed – some form of karma or cosmic justice.

Some wounds, though, never heal.

~

8

BOGART

They don't make movies like they used to.

I reckon that's true now, and we were quite adamant that it was true back in the late 70s and early 80s. It was the time of the Big Movie. Disaster pics with all-star casts were on their way out. Science fiction Blockbusters were the new thing. Leavening those were the Earnest Family Dramas. Movies about divorce, failed relationships, and the terrible sentimentality of ageing.

With the benefit of hindsight, some of the films I decried at the time of their release turned out to be good, even excellent, especially in comparison to some of what came after. At the time though, altogether too many new releases felt like 'populist pap' made to pander to the undiscerning masses, giving people what they were told they wanted.

That was the sort of rant that Beeb and I would sometimes share over coffee in the Refectory, or bourbon in the Student Club. Were we snobs? Probably, although at the time I'm sure we didn't think so. But whatever our criticisms, we did both enjoy going to the movies. It was very rarely a shared experience for us though. Beeb preferred to immerse himself in a film in solitude, without the distraction of company. I preferred to have someone with me, preferably somebody female that I fancied and who had some interest in me. Well, I *was* eighteen and prone to being driven by hormones.

Sometimes the cinema was simply a place for 'making out'. It was dark, comfortable, and gave an illusion of privacy. If you chose the right film and the right session, you and your companion may have the whole place to yourselves, or close to it. There were some movies I know I went to that I saw nothing of past the opening credits.

I don't think that was ever the case with Writer Jane and I. Oh, we shared a few nice moments of intimacy in dark back rows, but we actually liked watching the movie. Fondness for cinema was one of the things we really shared – both loving a good story, well told.

She was 'Writer Jane' because by odd circumstance, I went out with a succession of girls who all shared the same first name. To avoid confusion in later conversations they were known as Surfer Jane, Poolroom Jane, Nurse Jane and Writer Jane. All to do with their habits, area of study, and/or where we hung out together.

Writer Jane was the last of the four to come into my life. Well, technically she was the first of the four, as we'd met in primary school ten years earlier. But we chanced to bump into each other in the Undergraduate Library, enjoyed the bump, and started to see a lot more of each other.

I'd not long broken up with Nurse Jane. We were still friends, but no longer romantically together. I freely admit to having several girl-friends, but not at the same time – call me old-fashioned. Nurse Jane had no such qualms, and eventually found her natural curiosity being impeded by my being "possessive" (which I never realised I was, but that's what I was told...). But as I say, we stayed friends for quite a while. Right up to the time she got seriously involved with a guy she was clearly very happy to be possessed by.

But at the time of this recollection, we were still getting on well. And Writer Jane didn't mind her predecessor's occasional presence. It was always in the company of other friends, and I'd made it as plain as I could that she (Writer Jane) held centre stage in my heart.

Several of us were having a late lunch in the Refectory. The usual rambling desultory conversations happened between mouthfuls of croissant, cake, coffee and cola. Review and commentary on lectures, tutorials and texts. Critiques of music old and new. General lamentations about the political state of the world, particularly our part of it.

Beeb was on the fringe of the conversations, skimming the newspaper without enthusiasm. Suddenly though he sat up, looking excited. He folded the paper and pushed it to the centre of the table, a long finger tapping an ad at the bottom of a page of the Entertainment section.

"This looks like fun!" he exclaimed.

We all looked – it wasn't often that Beeb expressed such a sentiment. The ad was for a special showing on the coming Thursday night at the Paddo Cinema of a Humphrey Bogart double: *The Oklahoma Kid* and *Casablanca*.

"Too good to miss!" Beeb said, a comment that got a round of nods from most of us.

Writer Jane and I were the first two to agree on the attractions of the quirky double bill. The Western we knew nothing about, beyond the two leading men (Bogart and Jimmy Cagney), but *Casablanca* was a much loved favourite for both of us. Not particularly because of its romantic story, but for the way the story was told and given life by the whole cast.

Nurse Jane was keen, as was JP Kilpatrick, an amiable Arts/Law student who was part of our vague amorphous group who hung around the campus together. He had a strange predilection for wearing a green cardigan, whatever the weather. The others at the table begged off, citing either a lack of funds or no great enthusiasm for our hero Humphrey.

The plan was made – the five of us would meet outside the cinema on Thursday evening, half an hour before the session time. And we'd make an occasion of it. Dress up a bit to make it special. Period costume was beyond what any of us could afford, but we wanted to look Nice.

Writer Jane and I enjoyed dinner at an affordable little Spanish restaurant beforehand, but were still first to arrive. Jane looked fabulous in white chiffon that seemed to float around her in the breeze as we stood out on the footpath. I didn't have a suit to wear, but I teamed black pants and a blue paisley silk shirt with a white waistcoat that was just the right shade to match my lady's dress.

Beeb and Nurse Jane turned up independently. My ex wore a beige evening dress that flattered her curves. My old mate was simply elegant. He still comfortably fitted into the black suit acquired for the school formal, but now it was worn with a white turtle-neck sweater. It worked perfectly with the colouring of his complexion and hair – he looked like he'd stepped out of a silent movie romance. We all stood around in the foyer, looking a million dollars, munching popcorn and Maltesers, and waiting for JP to appear.

He never did. Days later he explained, red-faced, that his Mum had made a lamb roast that he couldn't say no to. We were more inclined to think he'd simply forgotten. JP's memory was notoriously dodgy. He'd missed more than one exam by forgetting the right time, date or place. Mind you, so had I, but that was because I'd had too much to drink. JP was just absent-minded.

Five minutes before the start of the first movie we made our way inside. It was a good crowd, but not a full house. That meant we could sit exactly where we chose, and there was only one choice for the four of us.

The Paddo Cinema was one of the great classic suburban picture houses that used to surround the Brisbane CBD. The Dawn in Chermside. The Lutwyche Imperial. The Palace, the Crystal, the Princess. Landmarks of my childhood, they were now in decline.

Gradually they died off, along with the Drive-In Movies, as the motion picture industry changed. Television took over, and video brought new release movies into the living rooms of the country. Cinemas became big 'multi-screen' places, with enormous screens and sound systems to match, ideal for blockbuster films that assaulted the senses like tidal waves of light, action and music. The humble local picture house, with velvet drapes, chintz wallpaper, maybe even still with a piano or organ sitting at the corner of the old stage, couldn't compete.

Some flirted with 'art house' cinema. Some tried specializing in the new R-rated movies that were just coming out – a niche market that rapidly filled with some of the worst films ever made. I remember my feet sticking to the carpet as I walked out of a shocker about an enormously-endowed female spy who had a secret camera implanted in her left breast (which was big enough to carry a camera, tape recorder, and probably a good-sized radio transmitter as well).

A few old picture houses were repurposed for a while as shops of various kinds. Eventually most were simply demolished to make way for shopping centres or glass-and-steel office monstrosities.

The Paddo at this time though was hanging on to its faded glory. It still had some period charm of earlier decades. The management were shrewd enough to keep the lights down so the frayed edges and worn patches weren't too obvious. This night's special double bill was part of a program intended to play up the history of popular movies, and with it the venue that had been their home in the Glory Days.

Most of the seats were red or brown leather, some cracking with age but still with an air of opulence. They weren't what we wanted, though. We headed straight for the front few rows: big canvas slings, almost like pale brown deckchairs! In times past, they were the Cheap Seats. Spending any length of time in them, with no real back support, craning your neck up to watch the screen looming in front of you would probably do terrible things to your spine. We didn't care. They were an important part of the experience as we stepped back in time. We kept a seat for PJ in case he turned up late, but happily settled ourselves in – Beeb and I in the middle, the two Janes on either side of us, and waited for the show to begin.

The cinema manager had arranged it well. He'd somehow sourced an old newsreel from the latter days of World War Two, and the evening opened with that. A mix of gung-ho propaganda and lightweight fluff that was the equivalent of the social pages of the newspaper, it was a ten-minute slice of nostalgic fun.

Then we launched into *The Oklahoma Kid*. Two of the great icons of gangster movies, exchanging the grimy streets and alleyways for the open range and the saloon. Released in 1939 it probably doesn't count as one of the great Westerns, but it was entertaining. How could it not be with Bogart and Cagney as stars?

Jimmy was the hero – the Kid of the title. Nominally an outlaw but really just a non-conformist, he gets off to a flying start by ambushing a gang of crooks who've just robbed a stagecoach and 'confiscating' their loot.

Resolutely and thoroughly nasty, Whip McCord (Bogey, of course!) moves on from stagecoach robbery to illegal land claim, running a crooked saloon, arranging the murder of one mayoral candidate and being responsible for the framing and lynching of another. The lynch mob's victim is the Kid's respectable and upright father, so the Kid rides in from the cabin he shares with some rough Mexicans to get his revenge. He picks off most of McCord's gang, leaving one alive to testify against his boss.

Finally, the Kid and his brother (the earnest, upright and colossally dull Sheriff Ned) confront McCord in his saloon. Whip shoots Ned. Cagney and Bogart fight, which is what we've all been waiting for. Bogart wins the brawl, but before he can finish off the hero he's shot down by the dying Ned. The Kid even gets the girl – his late brother's fiancée (coincidentally named Jane) decides she really likes the 'bad' brother and dupes him into marriage before he can dash off to the wilds of Arizona.

Like I said, it's not one of the greats. But it was fun, and the four of us enjoyed the romp. After the lights came up we lazed in our canvas chairs for a bit, discussing whether that counted as a 'happy ending'.

"It was for Jane," observed Nurse Jane.

"Do you think so?" mused Beeb. "Surely it wouldn't last. Would they really be compatible? He wasn't quite a willing husband."

Writer Jane, whose ambition was to pen The Great Australian Romance, replied, "It's a long-standing convention that opposites attract. Good girls go for bad boys and vice versa."

She was gently squeezing my hand as she said this. I was flattered, although looking back, I'm not sure which way around she actually envisaged the two of us. Her eventual husband was a very proper fellow from a good family, with a respectable professional career ahead of him.

Suddenly the cinema's Intermission entertainment kicked into life. First came the music. We might have hoped for some big band stuff of the appropriate era, but what we got was considerably more eccentric. It was the album of Jon English's Greatest Hits, recorded at $33^{1/3}$ rpm, but played at 45. It sounded like Alvin the Chipmunk singing *Behind Blue Eyes*. The absurdity of that voice delivering "no-one knows what it's like to be the bad man" in high-speed falsetto piqued my sense of humour. I'd love to know what the projectionist, or whoever made the decision, had been smoking.

Then the house lights dimmed to half, the curtains reopened, and a series of slides came on the screen. They were advertising a range of products from the period of the films. All the more reason to have used the music of Tommy Dorsey or Glenn Miller I'd have thought, but there you are. No accounting for taste. I was happy with the weird choice, although some of the audience were less enthusiastic.

Nurse Jane thought it spoiled the mood. Writer Jane called it "whimsical but strange". Beeb considered the "gratuitous oddity" of it worthy of me. I took that as a compliment, although it may not have been entirely meant as such.

The colours had been retouched in some of the slides, making them a little more garish than originally intended. There were ads for soap flakes, the Phoenix vacuum cleaner, the new model Riley roadster, some dubious pharmaceuticals, and a couple of long-vanished department stores. I remembered Bayards being my mother's first choice for buying fabric on her twice-a-year trip "into town" from suburbia when I was much younger.

A slide came up advertising Jaffas – the little chocolate balls with a crisp orange coating. We all looked at each other and nodded. All four of us went to struggle up out of our canvas slings to rush for the snack bar before the main feature started.

"Wait a minute. We don't want to lose these seats to anyone else during intermission," I said.

"I'll wait here until you get back," Nurse Jane promptly announced, and sat back down. She did better than that, draping herself languorously across all four seats. It was an effective impression of a Greta Garbo pose. The girl did have a certain style.

Returning laden with bags of lollies and cans of soft drink, Beeb and I were left to preserve our seats while the two Janes headed for the Ladies' Room.

"Why do they always do that in packs? Women, going to the toilet, I mean," I idly wondered, not expecting an answer.

"The popular view is that it's an opportunity to share gossip," said Beeb. "But I'm inclined to a more charitable view that it's a way of looking out for each other."

"A sort of mutual protection? Whereas us blokes are more ruggedly independent," I said with a smile.

"Mm. I don't know about that. Not just protection, either. Remember, we use troughs, they're confined to cubicles. I'm sure that having someone handy to toss in tissues or a new roll of paper must sometimes be very welcome."

I never have discovered the real reason for that common behaviour – no woman in my life has ever revealed what is apparently a tribal secret. But Beeb's suggestion still seems plausible to me.

The Janes returned just in time for the opening credits. If they had been comparing notes about me, as I secretly and egocentrically wondered, they gave no indication of it. Writer Jane snuggled into position with her head on my shoulder and my arm around her.

The four of us weren't the only patrons enjoying a 'retro' experience. I'd wondered about the little rattling noises that seemed to be coming from under us, until I felt something small go *plunk* against the back of my shoe. I reached down and found a Jaffa. Someone behind us was amusing themselves by rolling the little orange balls down the Paddo's sloping floor. A waste of good chocolate, I thought. The dear lady at my side was quite adamant that I wasn't to eat any of the bounty at our feet, though.

As I said, *Casablanca* was a long-time favourite for us. We'd all seen it multiple times. Enough to know a lot of the dialogue by heart. We couldn't help ourselves – we started to recite some of the lines along with Humphrey, Ingrid, Peter, Claude and the others.

The girls mostly managed to keep their voices down, although the collective singing of Le Marseilles got a bit boisterous. I'm afraid that both my volume and Beeb's crept up a bit as the movie went on, though.

"Rick, Rick, you've got to help me Rick!"

"You played it for her, now play it for me. Play it, Sam!"

"Here's lookin' at you, kid."

"Is that the sound of cannons, or the pounding of my heart?" Neither of us sounded remotely like Ingrid Bergmann.

"Shut up, you two!" came a harsh whisper from somewhere behind us. The annoyance was emphasized by an empty lemonade can bouncing off the top of the seats just above our heads. Luckily both of us were slumped low enough not to present any better target.

I chuckled. Beeb had the grace to look embarrassed and reply, "Sorry!" in a loud whisper.

"You probably did deserve that, you know," admonished Writer Jane softly, although she was smiling as she said it. And her voice was there with the rest of us (a good percentage of the audience, in fact) singing *As Time Goes By*.

"You know, Louis, this could be the start of a beautiful friendship."

We all joined in that memorable closing line, although we were diplomatically quieter now. I remember thinking, or at least hoping, how prophetic the words were for the four of us. I got that wrong, unfortunately, but it was a nice idea at the time.

Back at the Refectory the next day, we reflected on the evening's entertainment, regaling a largish group of lunchtime companions with recreations of scenes from both movies. I resisted any urge to try to duplicate the accelerated Jon English vocals.

It led into discussion of other movies, old and new, and what did actually constitute a 'classic'.

Commercial success? Critical acclaim? Winning lots of awards?

"Something that stands the test of time," suggested someone in the group, who then couldn't quite explain what that meant.

"Being memorable," said Writer Jane.

"Of all the gin joints in all the towns in all the world, she has to walk into mine," chorused those of us who'd been at the Paddo the night before, plus a couple of others.

"There's classics within genres," I proposed. "Films that typify what's best, or most distinctive, about that sort of movie. *The Magnificent Seven* for Westerns. *Psycho* for thrillers."

"*Gone With The Wind* for romance, *The Sound Of Music* for musicals," suggested Nurse Jane.

"I was never fond of that," I admitted. "Give me *Beach Blanket Bingo* any day."

"Frankie Avalon and Annette Funicello?!" cried Beeb in mock horror. "Seriously though, Paddy – that's the problem with your suggestion. Define 'best'. It's too subjective."

"How about influence?" asked JP. "A movie that other film makers want to duplicate."

"The style, or the success?" someone asked.

"Probably both!" he laughed.

"There are already movies being made in the image of *Star Wars*, or even *Jaws*," I pointed out. "Are you going to call them classics?" The disparagement of the 'populist pap' was clear in my voice.

"A long time ago, in a galaxy far, far away..." said Writer Jane, a few voices joining her for the second part of the line.

JP and several others then began making, "Bom bom, bom bom, bom bom," noises, evoking the soundtrack of the 'big shark movie'.

Beeb nodded thoughtfully. "Both instantly recognizable. Paddy, we might have to consider the possibility that mainstream popularity is at least one of the keys to a movie being a 'classic', whether you or I like it or not."

"It's called 'popular culture' for a reason, babe," Writer Jane told me, patting my hand sympathetically.

"Hmph. Culture is what germs get grown in," I replied, deliberately difficult.

Several people laughed. Beeb, though wasn't among them.

"Not just germs, Paddy. Life. Life grows in a culture."

9

BREAD

There are a lot of distractions in the life of a Uni student. Many, but not all, are self-imposed, and arguably many can be overcome by "a bit of self-discipline". Yes, that's an observation that I heard variations of from parents, lecturers, tutors, and well-meaning friends over the years.

It's an observation that I always found self-righteous, smug and inaccurate, certainly in my case. There can be lots of reasons underlying distractions. Some to do with motivation, some to do with preferences of where to direct attention. Sometimes it's necessity. The necessity of having a decent roof over your head, and having enough to eat and drink.

For many, living frugally was routine. Social life was carefully budgeted for. Any restaurant more up-market than the Uni refectory or the daily special Counter Lunch at a nearby pub was something to be aspired to for special occasions. Grocery shopping was predicated on prices, and was more often about 'need' than 'want'. If alcohol was important (and I wasn't the only student for whom that was the case) then value was more important than top-shelf quality.

That didn't always mean settling for 'cheap and nasty', in either food or drink, but it did mean doing the maths. Quantity for the dollars spent, presuming an acceptable standard of quality. Compromises were made. One mate of mine smoked appallingly rough, dirt cheap tobacco (possibly with real dirt in it), so he could afford a carton of beer per week. The beer and smokes were a priority for him – they got him through his week. Others bought less or inferior breakfast stuff so they could keep ice cream in the freezer and chocolate topping in the cupboard.

A few folks I know went vegetarian, not because of any philosophical or 'healthy' reasons, but simply because it was cheaper. Mashed spuds and tomato sauce never seemed like a meal to me, but I knew one group house where it was standard fare.

Much of this parsimony came about because of the inadequacy of the Tertiary Allowance provided by the government. It was intended to give the next generation of professional, business and political leaders enough to live on while we were trained to make our future contributions to society. Somehow the notion that tertiary education was an investment in the country's future was vanishing. Students were an inconvenience, and would soon be re-imagined again as a financial resource, both for the government and the institutions themselves as fees ramped up and the Higher Education 'Contribution' Scheme saddled students with debts that, for some, took decades to repay.

Some were lucky enough to have supportive families, sufficiently well-off to provide for their aspiring doctor/lawyer/teacher/engineer/nurse. Such generosity may or may not come with strings attached, of course. Even so, it was a situation sometimes looked on enviously by those of us in more 'independent' situations.

By the second year of his Uni days, Beeb was one of the luckier ones. His parents, after paying for his schooling, continued to support him. He still had the beige Datsun, unglamorous but functional. He'd moved out of the big rented house ("I was rattling around on my own in there like a pebble in a shoebox, Paddy.") and gone back to living at home, but effectively as an independent adult. His folks provided a small fortnightly allowance that supplemented the government's handout, and with no rent to pay he was substantially better off than many of us. Aware of his good fortune, Beeb insisted on paying for his own groceries and petrol.

The artistically-minded parents seemed to put few, if any, restrictions on their son's life. "They've become more like housemates," he'd say. Sometimes he said it almost wistfully, I thought. To the point where I wondered if he pined for, or was at least curious about, the more conventional hierarchical parental relationships most of his peers had.

"You're far better off without the conflicts," I warned him. "The pressure of expectations is a drag."

"Oh, I get those!" he hastened to reassure me.

"Behavioral, not just academic," I expanded. Even at school I'd learned a bit about his domestic situation. "You've been spared curfews, attempts at dress and haircut restrictions, commentary on friends and girlfriends, control of your eating and drinking or any other habits..."

My own mother was convinced that, as a long-haired Arts student, I *must* be 'doing drugs'. She'd heard all about it on talk-back radio, and nothing I said would change her firm belief that it was so. I got so sick of the accusation that I did eventually try a few different substances, figuring that if I was presumed guilty anyway I may as well do the deed. (Oddly though, none of the things I tried gave me any greater pleasure than alcohol. That was handy, because booze was cheaper, easier to obtain, and possession of it usually carried no risk of penalty.) The frequent arguments about my assumed 'habit' had much to do with my leaving home when I did – a wise move for my relationship with my parents as absence did, indeed, make the heart grow fonder. Eventually.

Beeb had taken my point, though, and did accept that he was in a better position than many of his peers. Then things changed, suddenly and dramatically.

Driving home from an art show one night, his parents were run off the road by a bunch of kids in a stolen car, at the front end of a "high speed pursuit" by a couple of police vehicles. The Bowmores' car rolled over an embankment at the side of the road, and immediately erupted in flames. It was thought it all happened too quickly for them to have suffered. That was the hope, certainly.

A misguided attempt was made to charge the young driver with murder. Intent could never be proved, of course, so that foundered. Even the lesser charge of manslaughter was rejected by the jury. Public dissatisfaction with the police force was already growing, and these twelve good persons and true apparently shared Beeb's view that the charges were a way of deflecting attention from the pursuing policemen's own culpability.

You might think that being orphaned overnight would improve Beeb's financial situation (if not his emotional one), but that turned out not to be the case. It was only after their shared funeral (a suitably interesting 'alternative' event I almost enjoyed, despite the circumstances) that he discovered that they had as many debts as they had assets. It turned out that at least some of that debt had been run up to pay for young Brandon's education. I'd landed in our esteemed school on a scholarship, but I knew the fees otherwise required were very high. Add the bills for top-of-the-line texts and compulsory uniforms and yeah, the cost of getting Beeb the best schooling they could conceive would have been high, and they'd still been paying for it when they died.

That realization hit Beeb hard. The guilt reaction was, initially at least, even stronger than the practical considerations of dealing with the inherited debts. Life insurance, and selling a lot of the 'goods and chattels', eventually cleared the amounts owing and left him with the house and basic furniture. And the beige Datsun, although it wasn't ageing well. More of Beeb's Tertiary Allowance went on the car's maintenance and running costs than the Council rates and other bills he was now responsible for.

I suggested to him that the house was big enough for him to rent out some of it. Share the electricity and other costs and improve his financial situation. I wasn't angling for a room myself. I'd not long moved out of the group house (Poolroom Jane and I having come to an amicable realization that we were better as friends than as a Couple) into a small but adequate one-bedroom flat, and was learning how to enjoy my own company. Furthermore, I'd known Beeb for what felt like a long time, and as fond as I was of him, wasn't sure how compatible we'd be as housemates.

It's strange. I was very conscious of the difference between his neat-and-tidy habits and my own far more casual attitude to domestrivia, and confident that it would jeopardize our friendship if we tried to cohabit. Yet I was somehow oblivious to the same fundamental difference with other people I tried living with over the years, notably a few ladies I was otherwise extremely fond of. Maybe love is blind, but friendship has eyes and some rational thought.

But Beeb rejected the idea. He said he valued his privacy too much, he'd seen too many instances of shared accommodation ending badly, and admitted that he tended to keep "unsociable" hours, often working in the early hours of the morning on assignments or some creative project of his own. I wondered, too, if the guilt he felt about his parents' revealed financial situation influenced his decision. It was 'their' place and having someone else live there might feel like some sort of betrayal. He didn't say that, as such, but I learned that he'd closed the door to their bedroom after cleaning it out, and simply never went in there.

I expected he'd eventually sell the house and buy somewhere that he could truly call "his own", but that never did happen. The place continued to settle around him like an old coat over the years.

As far as finances went, though, Beeb was now in a similar position to many of his peers. Rent. Food. Drink. Transport. Hopes of having "a life". When the Tertiary Allowance wasn't enough to make ends meet, many of us at Uni were obliged to take on whatever work we could find. It made us vulnerable to exploitation, but also threw up some weird and wonderful, and sometimes woeful situations.

Fruit picking was one of the casual employment options that often got touted as 'ideal for students'. I never quite understood that proposition. There was no such work available conveniently close to Brisbane. Travel was necessary, to wherever in the country the opportunity existed, and that was an up-front cost. More critically, it was seasonal work, and there were few picking seasons of any crop that coincided with the only long break in the Uni year, on either side of Christmas.

If you really wanted to make any decent money picking fruit (and the rates weren't brilliant, especially for inexperienced pickers who didn't know the tricks of harvesting really big quantities of produce) it was a challenge. It was necessary to abandon several weeks of lectures and tutorials mid-semester, find your way out to wherever the crop was grown, live as cheaply as possible while you were there, possibly still paying to maintain your accommodation back in Brisbane, work long hours in a demanding job you only *might* have been adequately trained to do, and then hope you would be paid enough to make the whole exercise worthwhile.

Door-to-door selling was another option. I had a go at that. Somehow, I talked myself into trying to sell vacuum cleaners.

Flogging cleaning products door to door was nothing new. I knew that brushes and brooms had been being sold that way for much of the century, in the US, at least. The Fuller Brush Company weren't the first or only, but for a while they were certainly the best known. There were a couple of movies: Red Skelton's *The Fuller Brush Man* made in 1948, and two years later *The Fuller Brush* Girl starring Lucille Ball. I remember watching both with my Dad on Sunday afternoon television when I was a kid. And there were a series of little pornographic cartoon booklets produced during the Great Depression.

The Adventures of a Fuller Brush Man comics had titles like "*Obliging Lady*", "*Dizzy Desires*" and "*Torrid Tess*". The art was scratchy but graphic. The stories (using the term loosely) were simple and, in my limited experience, completely unrealistic. If Brisbane had any attractive, bored, oversexed housewives desperately craving carnal satisfaction from any male who turned up at their front door, I neither saw nor heard any evidence of them.

Maybe vacuum cleaners were less glamorous than brushware. Certainly, judging by anything I've read about the Fuller Brush Company (the genuine one, not the porn version) their professional standards were a lot better than what I blundered into.

Our two days of 'training' should have been all the warning I needed. A half-day or less of being introduced to The Product. "Plug it into the wall with this lead, then press this button," was most of it. The other half-dozen recruits and I were shown the three or four Attachments that came as standard, and given almost no instruction on what to do in case of any technical or mechanical trouble.

The rest of the time, and pretty much all of the emphasis, was on hardcore selling techniques. How to get in the door, and more importantly how to get people to buy, immediately, before they had time to think.

Speed was essential, so the customer didn't have time or opportunity to do anything sensible like shop around. I'm not saying the machines we were selling weren't good. They were quite powerful and efficient, and no noisier than most similar equipment (as Linus once said in a *Peanuts* strip, "You'd be noisy too if you were being pushed around a carpet on your face"). What they also were, though, was unconscionably expensive. Way dearer than comparable options readily found in stores. Dear enough that 'we' offered a convenient payment plan. Well, it was convenient for the company, given it had the net effect of greatly increasing the purchase price, as anyone with even a rudimentary grasp of arithmetic would soon figure out. (Unsurprisingly, the salesperson's commission didn't improve on a 'payment plan' sale.)

The high pressure 'pitch' was quite effective on the new recruits, too. Although I don't think any of us were silly enough to buy a cleaner there and then, with the cost to be deducted from our future commissions, we were all gung-ho to get out on the road and make some money.

I can't speak for the rest of that 'intake', but I know that quickly wore off for me. Just about the first time I got through someone's front door and delivered my spiel. Oh, the demonstration was effective enough. The lady in question got her lounge room carpet cleaned, and a mattress as well, as a bonus. There was ample evidence that my nifty machine had extracted a whole lot of dust, dead skin cells, hair etc. that she hadn't realised were lurking within the fibres. But I still remember the look of shock on her face when I mentioned the price. And as I tried to pitch the payment plan option, I actually listened to myself and knew I couldn't sell it convincingly. Not if I wanted to sleep well that night.

I managed another couple of visits. The company didn't offer 'leads' for us – we had to arrange them ourselves. I knew a very small number of people who had cleaning issues, so I called on them, not to try to sell them a vacuum cleaner, but to help resolve a problem. For example, a couple of students moving out of their flat who couldn't afford a professional cleaner. Their carpets were left looking good enough to get their bond back without demur, which I suppose is testimony to the quality of the machine.

There was no surprise expressed when I returned my 'demonstrator model' back to HQ, together with my mint-condition order book. I suspect that happened a lot. Perhaps some of the sales force actually made money. It would never be me – the best I can say for the experience is that it sparked a type of conscience in me that I hadn't previously seen much of.

Other types of door-to-door selling were just as unsatisfying. Both Nurse Jane and JP Kilpatrick answered an ad in the classifieds that saw them spending a mid-semester vacation trying to flog 'Fine Art Prints' to households that were never likely to be appreciative.

They went from house to house with their portfolios of samples, "art for all tastes". Meaning: everything from classical landscapes and still lifes, to abstract geometric colour swatches, to the consciously cute or kitsch. Animals in hats and vests playing cards, waifs with unnaturally large limpid eyes, even a garish Jesus on a velvet background. And of course, the Order Book, so the customer could pay their substantial deposit, and COD the balance when the desired prints arrived. If they ever did – I couldn't say.

Given what I saw of this particular company's ethics, I'd be surprised if any orders that actually got placed were ever fulfilled. I know JP and Jane found themselves stranded in a little country town in Central Queensland with two changes of clothes and the folios of samples they'd been sent there with. The weekly 'retainer' they'd been promised, to be supplemented by 'the generous commissions on offer', never materialized in their bank accounts. Neither did any form of assistance to get home. Their calls to Head Office went unanswered.

Unwilling to cop any "I told you so" comments from family, and aware that their friends were no more financially sound than they were, the pair hitch-hiked back to Brisbane. Jane felt safer doing so in company with JP, although in truth she'd probably have been better able to look after herself than he would, if there'd been any trouble. I don't know that hitching was any safer back then than it is now, but it was a lot more common. Social and other media have made the dangers better known. The number of real nutters and psychos probably hasn't gone up, but their deeds have had a lot more publicity.

That sort of working environment was never going to appeal to Beeb. Between the lack of certainty of income, and the intrinsic awkwardness of 'cold calling', he ruled out that option the first time he heard it being mooted in the Refectory.

Instead, he managed to land an evening job in one of the many Italian restaurants in town. He'd have preferred French, but there were far fewer of those. He'd avoided an actual 'service' position, fetching food and drink for ungrateful customers, many of whom were routinely too drunk or thick to be Right even some of the time. Always Right is fine in theory, but it's hard to smile patiently at someone who complains that "there's tomato in this bolognaise" or that they'd "ordered a caber-nett savvy-non, but *this* wine you brought me is red!".

He got to stay in the kitchen, where, he hoped, he might eventually get to contribute to the actual preparation of food. That had been the promise when he started – 'do a good job and we'll offer you training as a chef'. The prospect of an apprenticeship at least intrigued him. It might be parlayed into a position in somewhere a bit more up-market, or with a cuisine that was more to his taste.

Alas, Beeb's experience turned out to have unfortunate similarities to those George Orwell related in *Down and Out in Paris and London* – coincidentally one of my old mate's textbooks at the time. The French term was *'plongeur'*, here it was 'kitchen hand'. Politely perhaps, a dishwasher, but the washing could extend to kitchen floors, walls and benchtops.

The only meaningful contact with food was when scraping its burnt form off pots and pans, dumping scraps into a bin, or scouring stains and traces from the plates and bowls which seemed to flow in endlessly from the tables throughout his entire shift. Exposure to decent wine was similarly confined to cleaning the remains from the glassware. Sometimes wine would be left in a bottle by a customer, but there was a hierarchy as to who might get to try such (deliberate or otherwise) generosity, and a dishwasher was at the very bottom rung of that ladder.

Beeb bore it with good grace for a while, tolerating the owner's casual bluster and the head chef's not-so-casual frequent rages and tirades.

"The ranting and raving is usually in Italian," he explained. "And it's rarely directed at me, unless I'm being uncommonly slow in having crockery washed and ready for re-use. I'm not important enough to attract much attention."

Unfortunately, high on the list of things the owner was casual about was the timely payment of wages. There was a peculiar inverse proportion happening: the lower the hourly rate, the less chance there seemed of actually being paid on the designated payday. Almost as high on the bossman's scale of disinterest was the notion of honouring promises made to new staff.

"I don't think it would make much difference though, Paddy," he told me over lunch one day. His voice was more tired than wistful as he explained that working alongside him at the kitchen sink most shifts was a fellow named Michael who was nearing the end of the first year of his apprenticeship.

"Maybe next year, you get to learn some sauces," he'd apparently been told. "Or maybe year after."

The prospect of years of washing dishes and scrubbing pots in a hot, noisy kitchen, for casual wages casually paid, wasn't one that cheered Beeb. Menial labour didn't bother him, but the real sense of being exploited, with little seeming likelihood of reward, did. I think he lasted four months (three more than I'd have surrendered) before leaving Michael to his sudsy duties. Hopefully that poor sod got a better offer soon after, or at least came to his senses and looked for other options!

There was one job that Beeb and I took on together. One of the local suburban shopping malls was having trouble with traffic flow in their sprawling outdoor car park. Customers were getting into the habit of parking wherever the hell they liked, especially at peak times like Thursday nights and Saturday mornings, so navigating around the place was regularly degenerating into chaos. Someone in management had realised that this wasn't good for business. The proposed solution was to have a team of 'security' staff on patrol.

Four of us were hired – one for each quadrant of the car park. Our selection criteria were twofold: be intelligent enough to hold a reasonable conversation with unreasonable customers, and be big enough to look intimidating when reasonable conversation failed. That was a key. Look intimidating, but not actually be intimidating. Look threatening, but never threaten.

Beeb and I ticked the appropriate boxes. Neither of us were small – my final belated growth spurt had got me to a size at which I could have played as a forward for the Uni rugby team had I been so inclined. And we could hold our own in an argument, sorry, *conversation* with a disgruntled car parker.

Our two colleagues were similarly well-qualified. Mark, also known as Tiny, was an engineering student who did play as a forward in his school's rugby First Fifteen. He was a lot brighter than he looked at first glance. At first glance he was a big lump of beef who probably still communicated in grunts, but he actually had a fine speaking voice and a great love of music. His car was an expensive sound system surrounded by rust, windscreens and four dodgy tyres.

Security Staffer #4 was a tall dark Italian named Leo. He often called himself 'Woggo', and invited the three of us to do likewise. He saw no offence in the nickname, taking it in the same spirit of casual mateship that sees "G'day, you old bastard!" accepted as an affectionate greeting rather than the precursor to a fight. Woggo studied accountancy and had some martial arts training he could fall back on if required. Much of his effectiveness in the job, though, came from his looking like a stereotype Sicilian gangster. It would have surprised no-one if he'd whipped out a stiletto for emphasis during the argument. The reality was far different of course, but he was happy to play up the image if necessary.

We were kitted out with white lab coats to identify our Official status. Fluorescent 'high-viz' vests hadn't been invented yet. Incongruous as the coats were, at least we looked a bit distinctive, and the capacious pockets proved good for holding food and drink.

Management did get the 'plausible threat' effect they desired. The coats disguised body shapes enough that 'big' just looked 'big' without inconveniently betraying muscularity or otherwise. Alongside the aforementioned Tiny and Woggo, Beeb and I completed the set. I'm told my scruffy hair and beard made me look like a dressed-up caveman. Beeb's broad-shouldered frame, dark hair and pale skin gave him some resemblance to Clark Kent without the glasses. And we all know who Clark Kent is without his glasses, don't we?

Despite the outdoor nature of our jobs, no sun protection was provided. We bought our own sunscreen and hats after the first Saturday morning. All four of us chanced to get broad-brimmed hats of different types. A straw hat for Beeb, a second-hand Stetson for me, Tiny wore a floppy cricket hat of the style favoured by some of the Aussie Test team, and Woggo bought himself a bushman's hat in camouflage-printed cotton. Upon seeing us together for the first time the Centre's office staff promptly christened us 'the Car Park Cowboys'.

It was seldom a difficult or demanding job. We'd each wander around our particular sector, nodding politely or chatting amiably with shoppers coming to or from their vehicles. If someone looked like parking in a clearly marked No Standing space, or somewhere even more ridiculous like in the middle of a lane between rows of spaces (it sounds absurd, but some people really did try to just stop their car and walk away because it was "close to the shop I want to go to – I won't be long") we'd wave them on. If they persisted we'd approach them before they got out of the car, or got far from it, and politely but firmly point out the error of their ways.

If we missed someone because we were in another part of our 'territory', or otherwise distracted, we'd leave a note on the windscreen. Something to the effect of, "Naughty, naughty, don't do it again or you'll be in trouble." It was a hollow threat, the four of us knew that. Nobody kept a record of the registration numbers of offending vehicles, and even if we did, the options were limited. In theory, Centre management could have a vehicle towed away for parking inappropriately (I don't know that it could be called 'illegally' on private property, you'd have to ask a lawyer) but getting the truck in and out when the place was already full of chaotic traffic would frankly have been more trouble than it was worth.

As I said, *seldom* difficult. Summer heat and humidity were unpleasant. Rainy days and evenings were inconvenient, especially as they prompted some drivers to be keener than usual to park close to the entrances to the mall, however problematical for anyone else. Genuinely confronting situations were mercifully rare.

There was the time that an impatient driver somehow managed to securely lodge the front of his Volvo in the side panel of a Council bus as the latter pulled into the car park. Getting the driver and his loudly annoyed partner out of the car was the easy bit. Trying to manage the traffic flow around the damaged bus (which had been pushed into the pole of a streetlight by the impact), both in the car park and out on the street, was far more challenging. Mobile phones weren't around, I couldn't get a message back to the office to call the police, and none of the increasingly irritated motorists seemed of a mind to help.

The bus driver managed to get in touch with his depot, and thanks to some evidently tortuous chain of communication, a police car arrived some fifteen minutes later (just after the required tow truck) and I was able to beat a tired retreat.

A little while later, a belligerent driver took umbrage at Beeb's request that he not park his station wagon across the entrance to a loading dock. Admittedly, he did eventually move his machine, but not before jumping out of it and landing a right cross on Beeb's jaw. It wasn't a great punch, and didn't do any significant damage, but it came as a real surprise. That, more than the force of the blow, deposited my old mate on his behind. He admitted later that it was more by good luck than good judgement that he didn't smack the back of his head on the bitumen. He had the presence of mind to roll out of the way as the offender, perhaps realising the stupidity of his actions, got back in his wagon and departed at speed.

Beeb also had the presence of mind to observe and memorize the registration plate that flashed past him. He risked management displeasure at abandoning his post, however briefly, to go to the office and report the incident, including the relevant rego number. One of the better office managers was on duty that day, and the promise was made to pass all the details on to the local police station.

That may or may not have actually happened. The local constabulary may not have been bothered to take it seriously, or perhaps they were busy with more pressing concerns. But Beeb never heard anything more about the incident.

That left a sour taste in the mouths of all four Carpark Cowboys, and frankly none of us were particularly distraught when Centre management decided that our services were no longer required. Peak shopping season had passed, so the numbers in the car park were down. Furthermore, we were all good at the job, so the difficulties had largely disappeared. Nobody in the office had the sense to realise that if the solution was removed, the problem was likely to soon recur.

Tiny, Woggo, Beeb and I all realised that. But none of us were inclined to argue. The conditions were only fair, the money barely that, and we all (naively) thought that we could doubtless do better.

I packed groceries for a while, standing at the back of a supermarket checkout and amusing myself by fitting as much as possible into a brown paper bag.

Those items were just being phased out as 'environmentally irresponsible' (save the trees!) and replaced by white plastic bags. Yes, the ones that are now decried as 'environmental vandalism', and rightly so.

Hardly the most interesting job in the world, but the pay was better than nothing. And I did enjoy a few months amorous involvement with one of the girls who worked the checkouts. Alas, Rita's family found a Uni student in their lives a bit intimidating. Multi-generational unemployment will do that. Rita's own position behind a cash register was loftier than her wastrel brother or usually-imprisoned father would ever manage, and was a source of immense pride for her dispirited mother.

For all that I tried, I couldn't find a decent conversation in that family. Rita and I had a nice physical thing going for a while, and she at least wanted to know more about stuff she didn't know about. But in the end, she toed the parental line that she should 'stick to her own kind'. I think she eventually married a guy who worked in a car wash. I hope they're happy.

If I was 'intimidating', then God only knows what Rita's family would have made of Beeb. Far more contemplative and philosophically inclined than I ever was. He'd landed in a better job than I did, too, post- our 'security' gig.

One of the shops in the mall whose car park we patrolled, was a bakery. It was actually the 'branch office' of a place that was operating very successfully in one of Brisbane's outer suburbs. So outer as to be on the edge of proper rural living. Brisbane was still sometimes called a 'big country town" in those days, and certainly there was farmland along some of its edges.

The bakery owners, Frank and Mavis, took Beeb on as manager, for the same hours as we'd patrolled the car park – Thursday nights and Saturday mornings. He was good, too. Good enough that they put him into the role full-time as soon as the semester ended. I think they had some notion that he'd be so grateful he'd stay on rather than return to his studies.

There were several reasons why that was never going to happen.

Beeb could overcome his intrinsic discomfort with the general public for a few hours per week, at a pinch, but a job in customer service wasn't a good fit.

A supervisory role was even less comfortable. The two teenaged girls under his charge found him "weird", so one of them told me. (Apparently his lack of interest in the Top 40 musical sensations that the girls were besotted with had something to do with that.) The much older woman who was the other team member was no happier. She simply didn't understand most of what Beeb talked about when he was trying to make conversation.

And more to the point, she'd expected to be given the manager's job simply because she was older. The preceding manager was an elderly woman who'd abruptly chosen to retire. Her own lack of understanding of even basic book-keeping procedures didn't strike her as a problem. So, she undertook a nasty little campaign of 'white-anting' Beeb to the business owners. A snipe here and a snipe there, about how he dealt with customers and staff. Some was exaggeration, but some, I'm confident, were total fiction. In a perverse way, I think he admired her efforts.

Ultimately though, the real problem was that he was too good at the job. He refused to sell stock that was past its best, despite the owners' imprecations. Frank and (especially) Mavis's view was that stale pies, cakes and bread should be given an 'extra day or three'.

Then, in an effort to boost the bakery's profile and public image, he offered some unsold goods to a charity who fed the homeless. Baked goods for those who'd truly battle to afford them. I knew about this because Beeb talked to me (the journalism student) about how to get some positive publicity.

The owners were livid when he told them.

"That's our pig food!" Mavis shouted.

Turns out they'd routinely pick up the designated bins where unsold stock was (eventually) deposited, out the back of the shop, and take them back to the property on the edge of town. Not for conventional disposal, but to feed the livestock.

More to the point, Beeb had managed to lift the shop's profile within the mall. He'd made the place look nice, set up the few tables and chairs so people might actually *want* to stop in and have a snack. Business was picking up. And *that* was the mistake.

A quiet conversation with Frank revealed all. He confessed to Beeb that he'd been quite content to be a pig farmer, but his wife wanted a more socially acceptable business. So, they'd started the bakery near the farm, and he'd been very surprised at how successful it was. So successful, in fact, that it threatened to muck up the carefully organized tax affairs of the piggery.

To offset the profits of the local store, they'd figured that the expense of a shop in a suburban mall, *bound* to be lost in the hubbub of surrounding competitors, *especially* if it was managed by incompetent amateurs like an old woman or an Arts student would compensate for the main bakery's income. It was meant to be a tax write-off.

"Sorry son, but you've made the place too successful. Do you reckon you could... tone it down a bit? I'll try to keep Mavis off your back."

"I'm sorry, sir, but I really don't think I can do a job without doing it to the best of my ability. You've got a good little business there, and it could really make a profit for you, if you let it. I'm not saying I want to manage it full-time, but I recognise its potential."

"Ah – afraid you'd say something like that. Seems like we'll have to let you go, Mr. Bowmore, but I do admire your principles."

Of course, admiration doesn't pay the bills. But Beeb took it on the chin, and resolved to live even more frugally, within the limits of the Tertiary Allowance. Something would turn up eventually.

And it did, as happened for many of us. A few days or weeks here and there, serving junk food or cleaning toilets, whenever a particularly difficult bill loomed. Swallow your pride and recognise that for some folks, this is what working life consists of.

At least we had hope.

～

10

BEACH

I t was a hot summer. Nothing new about that in Brisbane. We were getting towards the end of the academic year, and feeling a bit overwhelmed by exams, assignments and tutorials that all seemed to be due at the same time.

'All-nighters' were a regular occurrence for me. Sitting at my type-writer, surrounded by piles of scribbled lecture notes, photocopied texts and scrawled drafts littering the desk and surrounding floor. It looked like there'd been an explosion in a paper factory. Completely ignoring all of the safety warnings, I'd pop several caffeine pills throughout the night as I ploughed through thousands of words on the nature of rhetoric, comparative philosophy, medieval politics, and/or the literature of ancient Rome.

The pills were less hard on the bladder than a caffeine-equivalent quantity of cups of coffee, and I kidded myself that the Vitamins in them (B1 and B3 if you're interested) were doing me some good. I was luckier than some folks. I didn't suffer from the accelerated heart rate or nausea or dehydration that vexed some users. But when I stopped after a few days of stimulated wakefulness I did crash from a great height, and had to try to sleep through a headache that felt like a tent peg being driven through my skull.

The more ordered mind of Beeb spared him from some of my academic chaos, although his assessment workload was pretty comparable. He was just better organized. And considerably better at starting and completing assignments on time. Not for him the delusional pleasure of the sound that deadlines made as they whistled by.

He was able to help me with one useful tip though. Invest time early on during the preparation phase in looking for commonalities. Use the same research and source materials for multiple projects. Sometimes I could twist that into writing very similar essays for completely different subjects – very much Beeb's specialty. At one point he used fundamentally the same 3000 words for two assignments, a tutorial, and an exam essay in four different subjects.

"It's not cheating. The facts and the arguments are just as valid in each instance. It's just a matter of shifting the emphasis, maybe the perspective. And tailoring the introduction and the conclusions for each topic," he explained.

I'm not entirely sure that all of our examiners would have agreed. Lecturers and tutors in different subjects would socialize together, even members of different Faculties, but it seemed they didn't communicate much with each other about the minutiae of marking papers. I suppose the Staff Club was somewhere to escape from the day-to-day work, and think/talk about anything else. A retreat. Much like the Student Club.

What the productivity and pressure and panic ultimately meant was that when the mad rush of assessments was over, we all needed a break.

One evening a little bunch of us gathered on the bank of University Lake . This man-made lagoon at the centre of the campus, fringed with grassy slopes and a scattering of shade trees, was a welcome oasis on many days and evenings. Picnics, quiet solitude for reading or contemplation, a place to converse or even cuddle in fresh air instead of our usual air-conditioned atmosphere.

This particular evening was the end of semester for all of us in this group – a mix of Arts, Law and Medicine students, together because we shared common interests and similar senses of humour.

Blankets were strewn on the grass, a few citronella candles in jars provided patches of light and feeble attempts to deter mosquitos, boxes of pizza and fried chicken provided most of the food.

The food was mostly washed down with wine. It was a lot cheaper than beer or spirits, was actually preferred by several of the girls (and a few of the guys), and easier to keep cold. It's not like anyone brought an esky full of ice to Uni, even on the last day of exams. Our trick was to submerge a flagon in the lake, with one end of a length of string tied securely around the neck and the other to a rock, big stick, or for the well-prepared, a tent peg. The still water kept the booze cold, and the string meant it could be hauled out without the need for anyone to get wet.

Our effective refrigeration technique was an important reason for preferring flagons to the casks that had come onto the market earlier in the decade. Four-litre casks were better value in terms of their cost:volume ratio, but weren't well suited to being handed around and swilled from – you had to have some sort of glass, or plastic tumbler, which was another thing to carry. And we soon learned that casks didn't work in the lake.

It wasn't so bad if you were drinking quickly. But if you were taking your time, enjoying food, music and other distractions between drinks, the water tended to have a bad effect on the container. The box itself, and the glue holding it together. On the first evening that we tried the Chateau Cardboard option we lost two of our three containers. The string pulled right through the soggy 'handle' of one. The quality of the cardboard of the second was a bit more robust, but its construction wasn't. The paste used on the box's seams evidently dissolved in a half hour or so. That string hauled in a limp mess of coloured card and left probably three litres of rough riesling in a bladder somewhere on the bottom of the lake, like a big silver sea slug. Wading into the lake, diving and foraging among the mud and water weeds, was a cold, wet waste of time. For all I know, those bladders were still there if and when they ever drained the lake to clean it.

Having learned from that experience, our semester ending event was fueled by flagons. A fairly even mix of rough whites and rougher reds. Chilling the latter in the water had the double advantage of killing some of the taste and conceding to the heat of the evening. Summer was arriving early, and warm wine wasn't welcome.

One of the girls had brought a portable cassette player to provide backing music. Unfortunately, she'd neglected to bring spare batteries, and after twenty minutes the speed had slowed even past the point of being funny. Much as we'd enjoyed *Freakin' At The Freakers' Ball*, when the soundtrack of *Grease* came out sounding like a funeral dirge it was time to hit the Stop button.

Happily, a Med student named Chip Reid lived in a College relatively near the lake, and had brought guitars. He and Beeb were the only two real players, but it meant that there was some accompaniment for the singalongs that stretched into the night. The 'playlist' reflected the lightheartedness of the occasion. There were lots of offerings from the *Monty Python* repertoire, Beatles' favourites and old show tunes. Of course, *As Time Goes By* got an airing, the mood getting quieter and more reflective, in some cases more romantic, as the night wore on and the contents of the flagons diminished. We almost but not quite slipped into maudlin as we finished with *The Carnival Is Over*. Well alright, we probably were a bit maudlin, but not consciously so.

It was still warm, even approaching midnight. Someone suggested that we ought to go to the beach.

"What – now?"

"Why not?"

"I haven't got anything to wear!"

"So?"

Slightly more sensible heads prevailed, but only on the basis that those who had available vehicles weren't willing to drive all the way to the Gold Coast at that hour, or after so much wine. But it *was* agreed that the idea was good, and seven of us made plans to get together after a few hours' sleep and head down 'The Coast'.

There was a little ditty being used as a promo by one of the local radio stations. It ran:

Goin' down to the beach again,

Gonna fight for a space again.
Gonna check out the women,
Maybe do some swimmin'.
G'day! 4IP...

I think we'd even reprised it in the course of the singalong. It all seemed like a good idea, especially in the prevailing weather. Even to the girls among the group.

The 'few hours sleep' proved a generous estimate. It was just short of lunchtime when the two vehicles arrived in the car park at Broadbeach. There were other beaches we could have chosen, but we knew this area pretty well, having been to several gigs at a nightclub just off the beach.

One of the conveyances was a decrepit mustard-yellow Toyota wagon owned and only sometimes driven by Eric Jones, a medical student more commonly known as 'Fish', as in 'drinks like a...'. Fish's fondness for alcohol was the main reason that numerous other people took turns at driving the old wagon. Said vehicle was named 'Gastro', a double play on words – 'gastropod' reflecting its usual snail-like speed, and 'gastric' reflecting its surprising and probably unhealthy fuel consumption.

Arriving in the wagon were four of the Medicine Faculty's finest: Fish, Darlene Brown and her Irish boyfriend Kerry Fitzgerald Callinan (KFC), and Chip Reid. The 'fast food' connection of nicknames was purely coincidental. Fish I've explained, and Kerry's initials simply were what they were. Chip got his moniker in his earliest days at Uni when his portly physique and oily skin prompted some unkind person to observe that he was "greasy and full of fat like a Greek chip shop". I'm pleased to say that he learned enough in his medical studies to change his diet and exercise habits quickly, and had soon lost weight and cleared up his complexion. The name stuck, though.

Darlene didn't have a nickname. I don't think she approved of them. KFC used the contraction 'Darl' a lot, but most of us gave him exclusive use of it.

The other car was the dark blue Mini Cooper that Beeb had

bought to replace his mother's unlamented beige Datsun. It was a snug but comfortable fit for three. I curled up into the back, while Beeb drove alongside my beloved Angela.

We'd met during production of a Classical Roman comedy (practical application of an Ancient History subject – an assessment type I particularly liked!), and quickly become An Item. When I'd mentioned our new relationship to Beeb earlier, confessing once more to 'serial monogamy', he'd sighed.

"So, this is the new one."

"This is The One," I averred seriously.

"Again?" he'd asked with a smile.

But even he admitted, it did seem serious. We hadn't quite moved in together yet, but each had a one-bedroom flat a couple of blocks (less than five minutes' walk) apart. Angela's was a tidy upper storey brick unit, mine was a fragment of an old plaster and weatherboard house known to visitors as The Heap. We were both still too smitten to see the obvious compatibility issue on the horizon.

No regular nickname for her either, although 'Mercy' got used a bit by some (as in angel o' mercy, get it?). It never really caught on, there being only one Angela in our wide circle of friends anyway.

Neither of the cars that conveyed us to the beach possessed air conditioning. Very few did in those days, and certainly not within our meagre budgets. We were doing well to afford running costs, even with petrol as cheap as it was then. (In a year or two the Treasurer, Mr. Howard, would decide that it didn't seem 'fair' that Australians paid less for fuel than the rest of the world, even though it was being found and produced here, and imposed a tax that jacked the price up considerably, to 21 cents per litre. That move, coincidentally I'm sure, raised an extra \$678 million in revenue for the government in its first year.) Our 'cooling system' was known as 180-degree flow-through, which meant driving with the windows down.

The resulting airflow did keep us from sweltering too much in the cars, but played merry hell with the long hair that most of us wore. As we stood in the car park we looked like an assembly of badly damaged birds' nests. Even Beeb's dense hair had been unable to defy the 100kph draught, the window-facing side standing up like a wall of shiny obsidian.

It was too hot for us to care. Too hot even to adjourn to the bar in the nearby shopping centre, as might otherwise have been our immediate destination. Priority #1 was to hit the water. A quick application of sunscreen, and that's exactly what we did. None of us were particularly adept 'water babies' – even Fish, whose nickname, as noted, referred to his drinking capacity not swimming ability. That didn't matter. We splashed about, some of us did some body surfing, others just wallowed.

Darlene wasn't keen to go out too far, so sat in the water where the incoming waves had broken and collapsed to shoulder height. KFC dutifully stayed at her side, only rarely going out a bit deeper to ride the remains of a swell back to her, but looking wistfully at his more adventurous mates.

I'd been standing at a point where I could let waves simply break over me, shifting left or right to avoid incoming body surfers. Then I noticed that Angela had got herself out past the line of the breakers, and remembered she had something of a phobia about getting water on her face – the result of being caught in a bad rip when very young, apparently. I promptly went out to keep her company, and we bobbed comfortably together, soon joined by Fish. We floated casually, Angela and I holding hands, heads just above the waterline, chatting amiably and wearing the broad grins of students who'd just finished a tough slog of exams and assignments and didn't currently care about the results.

Chip and Beeb were body surfing, or attempting to, but having fun in the efforts. It was probably the most energetic I'd seen Beeb in years, if ever. He hadn't been a noted sports participant at school, only getting involved as much as obliged to. Walking had always been his 'thing', done at a pace that was comfortable, not competitive.

We carried on for over half an hour, I suspect, before deciding that we'd probably had enough UV radiation for a while. There wasn't a "bronzed Aussie" amongst us. Chip had the darkest complexion, which only means he was the least pale of seven.

The towels we'd brought were piled on the sand. We spread them out, and lay on the beach just long enough to be sun-dried. And that didn't take long on this scorching day.

"Time for a drink?" asked Fish.

Nobody argued, although it was politely, but firmly, pointed out that food was a necessary accompaniment.

For lunch, we hit the big shopping centre, only a block from the beach. It had a bar, a good range of food options, lots of shops that especially appealed to Angela and Darlene, and it was air conditioned.

The bar was packed. The seven of us crowded around a table built for four. When a big bowl of chips, another of salad, and a basket of garlic bread arrived, our only option was to hold a drink in one hand and eat with the other.

While we ate and drank, we talked. The place was too crowded, and too loud, for a seven-way conversation so we talked in twos and threes. Maybe it was a reaction to the whole end-of-semester vibe, but much of the chat was more serious than usual. Independently of each other, first Beeb and then Angela both asked me, "What do you want to do with your life?"

I really had no coherent answer. With Beeb, I turned the question back on him. "No idea yet," I said. "What about you?"

"Still thinking about it. A year of Honours if I can get into it – give me another twelve months to stall a decision."

My reply to Angela was, at least, more heartfelt if not more considered. "Spend it with you, my love." Yeah, I admit it, I was a hopeless romantic.

"Is that a proposal?"

I paused, and considered. "I reckon it might be," I said, taking her hand.

She squeezed my fingers, and eventually replied, "Not just yet."

"Did I miss something?" interrupted Chip, cheerily.

"No mate. Not yet," I said, as Angela and I both smiled at him, leaving him wondering.

Beeb had heard the whole quiet exchange, but said nothing. He'd raised an eyebrow briefly, but promptly taken refuge behind a half bourbon and soda. Whether he approved or not was impossible for me to read. I figured he'd tell me later.

Lunch complete, the medical students amongst the group insisted that it would be unwise for us to immediately go back into the water. Well actually, it was Darlene Brown who insisted – the others agreed out of diplomacy. Angela was quick to agree, too. The alternative was shopping, not always her favourite pastime, but these weren't her usual stores.

One of the last to be visited was a surfwear shop. Lots of colourful boardshorts, t-shirts, wet-suits for the guys. Much the same for the girls, with shorts instead of boardies, and a big range of 'swimming' costumes in various degrees of skimpiness. Some of them seemed very purposefully designed *not* to be worn in the surf.

Among the items on display was a brief, but very pretty bikini. A few scraps of bright tropical-print material, held together with white string.

I gave Angela a hug and playfully said, "You'd look great in that, beautiful."

She blushed and laughed. "Oh, no I wouldn't. I haven't got the figure for it."

Darleen had turned up her nose at the outfit, saying , "Oh, you wouldn't see *me* in that!"

I think all of us, except (possibly) KFC, breathed a discreet silent sigh of relief. Darlene had been undiplomatically, but not unreasonably, described by another medical student as having "childbearing hips that went all the way up to her armpits".

Angela, however, was mostly slender with a slight tendency to what I'm told is described as 'pear-shaped'. The bottom part of the pear was still very trim though. She had a sister who was a year younger, and a lot more voluptuously endowed. I think my lovely lady had felt on the wrong side of comparisons for a while. She'd come to the beach with a one-piece blue costume that was made from a nice enough fabric, but wasn't cut to particularly flatter her, worn under a loose t-shirt and shorts.

She sighed slightly as she looked at the bikini, and shook her head again.

"My body wouldn't do it justice," she said, a little wistfully.

I didn't want to seem pushy and argue, so I moved on. Beeb, though, laid a gentle hand on Angela's arm and leaned in to stop her and talk to her quietly. So quietly that I missed it. Only later did Angela relate to me what he'd said.

"Funny thing, body image. Self-awareness is one thing, self-criticism is quite another. If you keep disagreeing with someone who says you're beautiful, there's a real risk that eventually they'll believe you, just from the force of repetition. I don't know how it works for you, but a man doesn't notice the imperfections in the woman he loves until the woman he loves points them out. And the more they're pointed out, the more they notice. Try to see yourself through his eyes. Accept it and appreciate it. If Paddy tells you you're beautiful, smile, hug him and say thanks, because he's telling you his truth." He paused and smiled. "And for what it's worth, I reckon he's right, too."

With a little nod he'd walked away, leaving her to cogitate.

One record shop and a shoe store later, we adjudged our lunch to be sufficiently digested to go back to the beach. There were a few shopping bags being carried among the group, and four of us now sported sun hats or caps for a bit of belated protection. We'd done our bit to support the local economy without being excessive. We were students – we couldn't spend excessively if we wanted to!

The shopping was stashed in the respective cars while the towels were taken back out, and we found a good-sized patch of sand to spread out on. T-shirts were removed ready for the application of another coat of sunscreen.

Angela was no longer wearing her one-piece. While nobody was watching she'd bought the bikini, and slipped into the changeroom to put it on. The blue outfit was discreetly tucked into the shopping bag in its place.

The effect was all she could have hoped for. I'd been right. She *did* look great. And it wasn't just me who said so, there was a chorus of approval (albeit with some considerable surprise) from the whole group.

Even Darlene managed a supportive smile. It can't have been an easy moment for her. KFC's reaction was as fulsome as the rest, and she must have been aware that comparison with Angela's suddenly very visible slim figure did her no favours. Her bright green plain one-piece made her look a bit like a Granny Smith apple with arms and legs.

Angela hugged first me, then Beeb. She planted a kiss on his cheek and whispered thanks in his ear, eliciting a very satisfied smile, before turning back to me and delivering a much longer and more romantic kiss. Then with a laugh she pirouetted and started to run down towards the sea. Impulsively she cartwheeled across a vacant stretch of sand, delighting in the feel of the warm air on her skin, and the admiring looks she knew she was attracting. The skimpy bits of white, blue and green cloth covered what was needed to be legal on a public beach, but only just.

I knew that Angela's sister had some reputation for being very uninhibited about her curvy body and possibly a bit generous with it (Darlene would have said 'promiscuous' but I'd have called that harsh). I knew that my girlfriend had felt overshadowed by more than just their physical differences, and just for once was revelling in not being the Good Girl. My lovely Angela felt daring, and attractive, neither of which happened often. The free-spirited cartwheel was an expression of that, and I approved for reasons far beyond the visual treat.

As her rival (who wasn't in that position at all, really) skipped away, Darlene's smile dissolved into an expression of disapproval that would have done credit to Queen Victoria. I only glimpsed it when Beeb nudged me and indicated in her direction. Everyone else was still watching Angela's frolics. My first thought was that it was less prudishness than jealousy, and as I said, it was hard not to feel at least a little sorry for her. But not enough to spoil my girl's moment.

We all headed for the water, and had at least as much fun as we'd had earlier in the day. Probably more, as the morning fog in some heads had cleared, and we were just appreciating a simply fabulous day. Angela's costume managed to hold up against the action of the waves – the strings were suitably snug. I have to say, though, that I very much enjoyed our embrace in the calmer water out past the breakers.

After the sea frolics came an hour or so on the sand. Beeb, KFC and the girls started out reading books and magazines they'd bought or brought, but soon joined the other three of us as we noisily constructed sand sculptures.

At one point, Chip stood in a generously proportioned hole that we dug, and posed patiently as we created the figure of a large scorpion around him. His head looked suitably bizarre protruding from the sandy carapace of his zodiac star-sign.

"It's a good thing you're not a Virgo," remarked Fish sagely.

"Not me!" laughed Chip.

"The sculpture could be interesting, but I don't think the head would look right," observed Beeb with mock seriousness.

"Hey – I'm a Virgo!" cried KFC suddenly.

"That would *not* look any better!" advised Darlene, by now relaxing back into the afternoon's spirit of fun.

We did contemplate a return to the bar later in the afternoon, but decided that would be unfair on our designated drivers. Better to head back up to Brisbane, and reconvene somewhere convenient there. There was a pub fairly central to our various homes. Not walking distance, but a much shorter and less risky drive.

I don't recollect that we stayed at the pub for long, in the end. A few drinks, good conversation, shared exhilaration at an excellent day that had strengthened bonds of mateship. Even Beeb was less conspicuously 'on the outer' than he usually positioned himself. I think Angela's low-key but genuine gratitude to him helped with that.

The bonhomie of that day probably contributed to the decision soon after to set up a new group house. Angela and I shared a rambling old somewhat run-down Queenslander with KFC, Darlene, and two other mutual friends: a music student from a band we liked, and another Arts student who was a would-be biker (no gang would have him).

Not a wise choice, really. It didn't last long. There were a few egos that would have eventually clashed anyway, but the ultra-conservative Darl didn't play well with others, especially others who didn't conform with her views of what was Right And Proper. Arguments very soon became frequent, and shrill, and we went our various ways, with Angela and I going back to separate but conveniently close flats for a while.

Darlene was blamed for the breakdown of the household, though in hindsight we should have known better. Even the good Catholic KFC would eventually have enough of being dominated, although not until after a few years of relentless marriage.

Beeb managed to resist saying, "I told you so". He was never going to try living in a group house. He was too entirely happy in his own company.

After the day at the beach came a round of end-of-year parties, Christmas parties, and who-needs-a-reason parties. Mostly all good fun, I think, although there's a certain amount of alcoholic haze overlaying the events.

The following year saw Beeb and I losing touch with each other. His decision to shoot for acceptance into Honours meant he took his study far more seriously, sometimes in the library, but far more commonly at home in splendid isolation with books and papers. His presence at the Refectory and the Student Club became increasingly rare.

Mine on the other hand escalated. I scraped through on my subjects, mostly. One or two decent successes, a greater number of crashing failures. My mind was usually on other things. One of them was Angela, and our pleasingly developing relationship.

Another was the theatre, as I got more involved on stage and off, willfully oblivious to the fact that the chances of my making any sort of living from the stage were, at best, remote. Like life with Angela, it was *fun*, and that's what mattered to me.

If I was asked again what I wanted to do with my life, I'd have answered, "Enjoy it."

On one of the rare occasions that I encountered Beeb towards the end of the year, he expressed a similar sentiment. I think we each had a quite different image of what that entailed, though, and I'm afraid neither image was especially practical or realistic.

BEYOND

11

BACKSTAGE

Our University days were well behind us, and we'd moved on in the world. Beeb and I had drifted further apart. We exchanged the occasional card and letter, however aside from well-intentioned but vague undertakings to 'catch up soon' we pretty much lost touch with each other's lives.

For a while I'd lived with Angela, first in a group house then on our own, like a real couple. It hadn't worked out. I think my novelty wore off for her, and while I still cared a lot for her, all the little niggles and irritations had become the more significant parts of our time together. When you start paying more attention to the 'bad' habits than the endearing moments, it's time to call it quits.

What had been my charming eccentricities had become aggravations to her. On the other side of the equation, her drive and focus that I'd admired became a barrier between us when my ambitions didn't keep pace with hers. Angela left me and followed a rapidly-rising management trajectory in the State Public Service. I muddled along, not looking much further ahead than my next meal and a drink.

I had actually managed to parlay my University education into a real job – no mean feat for a Bachelor of Arts, even then. I was working for one of the small suburban newspapers that were still sprinkled around Brisbane then. Looking back, it would be overstating it to call it a 'career in journalism'.

My role was to report on local events. The local sporting teams routinely submitted match reports and results, which I dutifully turned into comprehensible English. A new shop, playground or even street might open, or an old favourite close. There might be a profile piece on some prominent local identity who'd won an award, or passed away after a life of dedicated service to something or other.

It was in pursuit of the latter type of story that my duties included a daily scanning of the classified ads pages of the *Courier-Mail*, the morning metropolitan newspaper in Brisbane. The 'hatch, match, and dispatch' columns as they were irreverently called. I had a card file of names of folks who already had some level of local notoriety, good or bad, and any news about them was an instant story. Maybe a filler, maybe even something more substantial.

During one morning's routine skimming of the obituary column I read Beeb's death notice. I pulled up short. Read, and reread, which didn't take long. There were no funeral details, just a stark message that Brandon Baxter Bowmore had died on the 31st of March.

Had I been thinking clearly, I might have considered it unusual, even for Beeb. There was no funeral director listed, no contact information.

I knew he had no siblings, and that his parents had died while we were at Uni. So, I grieved alone. Well, almost.

I got an unexpected phone call from Nurse Jane, now married and working in a regional hospital up north. She happened to have seen the terse notice while glancing at the paper in the staff lunch room. Apparently reading the obits is a bit of a habit for some nurses, keeping an eye out for ex-patients they'd become attached to. Jane still had my number (to my surprise) and wanted to check that I knew, and was okay. We chatted for a while, reminiscing about Beeb, and inevitably about Us.

She apologised for not being able to get down to Brisbane for the service, assuming I must know more than was in the ad. When I explained that I knew exactly as much as she did, she was as puzzled as I had been.

"He always was a loner," she said. "I guess he carried that through, right to the last."

"I suppose so," I replied, touched by her sympathy, but realising I didn't want to say or hear much more.

We said a rather fond farewell. I took an early, and long, lunch, which mostly came in a series of glasses. I wasn't very productive that afternoon. To be honest, I was probably less productive than usual for the rest of the week. A lot of vodka will do that.

Months later I fronted up at an AMUSE (Artists and Musicians United for Safe Energy) fundraising show at a conference centre in Spring Hill that had been awkwardly converted into a concert venue. It was only modestly sized, and acoustically dodgy – of necessity, amplifier volumes couldn't go too high or whatever was being played turned into the aural equivalent of pea soup – but it was, in real estate sales terms, 'intimate'. 150 people would have been a packed house.

AMUSE was a well-intentioned body that grew out of the anti-nuclear protest movement that still had good traction at the time. An effort to prove that there was more to the movement than demonstrations and street marches that inevitably ended in confrontations with the police, arrests and violence. I remembered those well from Uni days, so I was always going to be a sympathetic audience and write a suitably enthusiastic, supportive article about creative energy being more powerful than any other kind. Nominally I was there to write a story on a local singer who my editor incorrectly thought was going to make a name for himself. My private agenda was to give AMUSE as a whole a decent plug, as their efforts at self-promotion didn't seem to have been all that successful. Certainly, the show I attended had drawn a lot less than a full house, even in that modest venue.

There was no program available, in advance or on the night. I assumed there must have been a running sheet for the stage manager to follow, and to keep the various acts running on time and in the correct order, but it wasn't shared with the small crowd. Not even an MC – whoever and whatever was coming up next was an ongoing mystery. I'd been tempted to use my Press Card as a backstage pass, just to get a few clues as to what was to come, but in the end, I decided to play it like one of the seventy or eighty punters and hope to enjoy the surprises.

By and large, I did. There was a woman who bore a distressing resemblance to the one who'd preceded Sky Blues at our Uni gig, vocally if not physically. I'm pleased to report that her annoyingly nasal tones were admirably compensated for by two other solo singers, one male and one female, who were both gentle balladeers. There was a five-piece reggae band who played with more energy than talent, but their enthusiasm was infectious. Judging by the kit (drums, amplifiers, and several mic stands) left lying about the stage, I figured there were more bands to come.

After the sweet-voiced Carly Simon-type singer took her bows and left the stage, there was only a brief pause as the lights dimmed and a single spot came back up to illuminate the stool that sat front and centre.

Out came the next act, to polite applause. A Performance Poet, managing to not look like a caricature of a Sixties beatnik, even in his black beret. The plain, open-necked white shirt and dark jeans let the focus be on the words, not the speaker. It was Beeb.

I don't think the first couple of poems actually registered with me. Astonishment isn't a strong enough word – I think I was in a state of at least mild shock.

Gradually his voice, sometimes soothing, sometimes impassioned, but always measured and resonant, managed to cut through my emotions. And man, there were a few of those. Relief wrestled with rage, bafflement, delight, intrigue. With an effort, I forced myself to Be A Journalist and focus on the performance.

His writing was as earnest as ever. Some of it was pretty accusatory, railing against disengagement and apathy, stopping just short of being aggressive. Other pieces were gentler exercises in storytelling, and I thought they were more effective for their lighter touch. What there wasn't, though, was humour. There was some effort to inject some light to throw the dark into relief, but it seemed he still couldn't bear the thought of anyone laughing at his work, even if they were meant to.

Beeb's delivery was well suited to the content. Without the constraint of a tune to carry, he just let the words find their own rhythm. And while he was never jovial, he varied his pitch and pace enough to keep himself easy on the ear. All up, it was as good a piece of serious performance poetry as you might hear, and he got a respectful audience, as he deserved.

Shrewdly, he didn't make it a long set. 'Recitation' is not an art form encountered very often, even then, and not as many people have the attention span to concentrate on verse without music as a few generations earlier. So, when he left the stage, it was to a good round of warm, if not rapturous, applause. Including mine.

And now I did use my Press Card. There wasn't exactly a 'security guard' protecting the backstage area, just a dark-haired girl in an AMUSE t-shirt, jeans and outsized work boots. She had a copy of the running sheet on a clipboard, and ticked off names as people presented themselves to her. My arrival was a surprise – she'd only been told to expect performers – but I clearly wasn't any sort of groupie or overenthusiastic fan, and she had the good sense to recognise Press = Publicity = Positive. She pointed me towards the changing room with a happy smile.

I found Beeb in front of a mirror, wiping off the light layer of stage makeup that had prevented his paler-than-ever skin from glowing unnaturally under the spotlight. I stood silently in the doorway for a moment, watching him, until he noticed me over his shoulder in the mirror.

"Paddy! Good to see you!" he said, casually cheerful.

"I thought you were dead!" I exclaimed. There was no cheeriness in my voice. "I read the notice in the paper!"

"Ah. Right. Um... Mark Twain. The reports of my death are greatly exaggerated, would you believe? Although I didn't think so at the time."

"You've lost me," I admitted.

"It was me that had that notice printed," Beeb admitted, with a degree of embarrassment.

Confusion, relief and anger grappled within me. "Why?" I managed.

"Because to me it seemed true. Very often, still does. I've joined the Public Service."

"Thousands of people do," I pointed out tersely.

Beeb nodded and tried to explain. "I can't do a job and not try to do it well. When I get home in the evenings I've got little or no energy left. I've never been much of a 'night person'. I haven't written anything worthwhile since April. At least you write for a living."

I gave a grim smile. What I wrote for the paper was hardly the sort of material Beeb loved to produce. It didn't even satisfy me, really.

I gestured towards the stage. "You're doing this."

"An unexpected one-off. I met one of the organizers in a coffee shop while he was sticking a little flyer in the window. Told him I was impressed by the idea of AMUSE, got to talking, and discovered they were still trying to pull together a program even though they were already advertising the show. I volunteered on the spur of the moment, and here I am. But none of that material is new. Even with the impetus of this performance, I couldn't create anything new that I was happy with."

"Maybe now you've had a taste of being in front of an audience, it'll come back to you."

He gave a wry smile. "I don't think the stage is my natural environment, old friend."

As we talked, another bloke ambled over to stand beside Beeb. He was quite short, and as lean as a ferret. Dark skin, long dark hair, and a beard that had been hacked short rather than trimmed. I recognised him as the percussionist from the reggae ensemble.

He dropped a long-fingered hand on Beeb's shoulder. "Really liked your work, man," he said, grinning broadly. "Wish I could write like that."

The poet gave an almost embarrassed smile in response. "Thanks, mate. You guys sounded good."

"Aw, we're just havin' some fun. Glad you liked it." He thrust out a hand. "Jimmie."

"Brandon Bowmore." With a look at me, he added, "Call me Beeb," as he shook Jimmie's hand.

I introduced myself, and at Jimmie's suggestion we relocated ourselves to the small bar that had been set up at the front of the venue. Several Eskys behind a trestle table, and a biscuit tin doing service as the till – but it was likely to be the most profitable part of the evening's operation, I suspected. While we stood there one of the AMUSE volunteers arrived with more cartons of beer and another two bottles of rum to restock, and I gathered that wasn't the only such run of the night.

The origin of Jimmie's accent had eluded me. He looked vaguely Aboriginal, played tom-toms like an African, and was dressed like a Jamaican. It turned out he was Sri Lankan. As he put it, he'd "bummed around the South Pacific for a few years" before settling down in Brisbane.

Sri Lankan, not Tamil, and absolutely 100% not the type of guy that Priti's mother would have had in mind. But he was genial and cheerful. His company helped smooth over any tensions that there might have been between Beeb and I, especially after a few drinks.

I did keep an eye and an ear on the rest of the show, but I already had most of what I needed for my story. The guy I was meant to be looking out for came and went. He proved a better guitarist than singer, and his songwriting skills came a distant third. His best work was cover material, particularly Don Maclean's stuff. For my editor's sake I'd be as positive as I could, but barring an accident or a miracle, I couldn't foresee a career beyond friends' parties and an occasional suburban pub gig, if he was lucky.

Even those seemed unlikely when Jimmie quietly observed, "Pain in the ass to try to work with. We offered him a chance to do a couple of songs with us, but he tossed us off – not his type, he reckoned."

The article in my head just became a little less positive.

Jimmie left us to join in a jam session to end the night, featuring musicians from several of the acts on the program. My 'local hero' wasn't among them (uninvited or refused, I never found out), and neither was Beeb. Not surprising, he was in the show as a poet – he'd apparently never even mentioned he could play the guitar.

We stood holding our drinks, watching the show wrap up.

"Could have been us up there, I suppose," I mused. "If we'd persisted."

Beeb seemed a million miles away. "No future in it," was the distant reply.

"Then, or now?" I asked.

There was a long silence. Both of us were tapping our feet in time to the music.

"Either. Both."

Part of me wanted to argue with the negative, dismissive sentiment, but I could hear the defeat in his voice. I thought of the 'obituary' he'd penned for himself. Maybe that had been the most creative thing he'd written in months.

"Write," I said. "Find time. Make time. Carry a notebook at work. Scribble when you're at lunch, or when you're on the bog, or between... between whatever it is you do at work. It doesn't matter if you're not satisfied with it. That's probably a good thing. It'll encourage you to do more, do better."

Beeb looked at me and gave another wry smile. "You reckon it's a matter of practice, eh Paddy?"

"Not practice. Discipline. As long as I've known you, you've had a head full of stuff worth writing down. I don't believe that's run out. Just don't give up on letting it out. Don't give up on *you*."

He tapped his beer can against mine in a small toast. "Thanks, old friend. I appreciate your confidence."

We hugged, not at all awkwardly, and made sincere but let's say, *optimistic* promises to keep in contact.

After the jam session finished, several of the musos joined us at the bar, revelling in mingling with an appreciative audience. A few attempted to buttonhole me, apparently thinking being "interviewed by a journalist" would help their careers. Thanks for that, Jimmie. I tried not to disillusion them, but I knew my suburban weekly wasn't *Rolling Stone* either. I'd submit a freelance story on the whole gig to the *Courier-Mail* and a couple of relevant magazines that I knew, but my hopes weren't high.

As it turned out, one of the magazines condensed what I'd written down to a paragraph or two in a generic regular 'what's been happening' feature. It gave AMUSE a little glint of publicity, but none of the performers got a helpful mention. I didn't get a by-line, either.

While I was having my ear bent by a loud young guitarist calling himself Billy Bee, I lost sight of Beeb. He'd slipped away into the night. By the time I got outside to look for him he'd disappeared from view. Walked, driven, hailed a taxi? No clue.

No chance of finding, or following him. I could only stand there in the dark, and wonder what direction he'd gone in.

12

BRETHREN

Now that I knew he was still numbered among the living, I did make some effort to stay in touch with my old friend. Correspondence turns out not to be my longest suit, unfortunately, and Beeb wasn't a lot better. We weren't ignoring each other, just inclined to be caught up in our own day-to-day *stuff*. But sometimes one or other of us would have a sudden moment of inspiration (or conscience?) and make contact.

One Saturday I rang to see if he'd be interested in joining me at a movie that night – some new release that sounded potentially interesting. As I later found out, the trailer was the best thing about it. Not the only instance of all of a film's best bits being taken out and assembled into three minutes, and you could comfortably miss the rest. But on this particular evening Beeb wasn't available.

"Ah, got a hot date lined up?" I said jokingly.

"Er... no. No, Paddy, something quite different." There was a momentary pause, as Beeb made up his mind to divulge his plans. "I'm speaking tonight."

"Cool! Performance poetry?"

"No, I'm the main speaker at a Christian Youth Fellowship meeting."

I was intrigued. "You've settled on a religion?"

"I'm experimenting."

That sounded more like it. "Tell me about it," I invited.

So, he explained to me some of the workings of the group he'd 'discovered'. Not the most conventional of the organized Christian religions, certainly not 'mainstream', which was entirely in character for Beeb.

"They get called 'Brethren', even by some people within the group, but I don't think that's really accurate. They're not dissimilar, but the true Brethren – the organized denomination using the name – only recognise the New Testament. The teachings of Jesus, and the instructions of Paul. These guys give primacy to those books, but also take the Old stuff as divinely inspired and important, too."

"I think I like the Brethren idea better," I remarked, remembering some of the dire things I'd heard contained in books like Leviticus – how people should be stoned or put to death for wearing the wrong fabric or having a skin condition or something that possibly made sense to somebody in Persia in 500 B.C. but which seemed bloody mad to me. Emphasis on 'bloody'.

"So, if not 'Brethren', what do these folks call themselves?" I continued.

"Just 'Christians'," he replied. "At most, 'evangelical Christians', as in, their primary responsibility is to spread the word of God."

In many ways the group were profoundly conservative. He conceded that they were inclined to be towards the far right of the political spectrum, which didn't sit well with him, but many of the people he'd met had a social conscience that was strangely at variance with their proclaimed politics.

One of the things that most fascinated Beeb was the Brethren's absolute rejection of anything that smacked of 'idolatry'. No religious icons to be seen – no statues of Crucified Christ, no Blessed Madonna, no paintings of the Stations of the Cross – not so much as a crucifix worn around the neck of the faithful. It was Christ that was worshipped, not the symbols. There seemed an honest simplicity about this that attracted him. I admit, I liked the idea too.

"They don't have a 'church' as such," Beeb explained. "They meet in something called a Gospel Hall. Each Hall has an assembly, but there's no over-arching church structure or hierarchy. They're all independent. I've visited a few different ones, and for all they have in common, they each seem to have their own character."

I'd often been bothered by the grandeur of church buildings, and by implication, the institution that they represented. "You want *us* to help the poor, tithe money to you, donate, donate, donate – while you sit in these flashy buildings, full of valuable ornaments, paying no taxes and liquidating none of these assets? I don't think so!" was my usual line of thinking, and that was before I had any grasp of things like the extraordinary value of the Vatican's treasures, for instance.

So, the 'no frills' attitude of the Brethren struck a sympathetic chord with both of us. And it was epitomized by the bloke who'd first sparked Beeb's interest – a guy he'd met at work named Kelly Holden.

"One of the most thoughtful people I've ever met," Beeb explained. "In both senses of the word. Thinks, *really* thinks deeply about a lot of things, and is also naturally kind and considerate."

"Too good to be true?" I mused aloud.

"I wondered about that when I first met him," Beeb admitted. "But I reckon he's genuine. It's not like he'll spinelessly agree with whatever anyone is saying, but he'll listen and respect their point of view. State his own case, but without making an argument of it."

I thought to myself how very unlike my old mate this character sounded, but I could hear the regard in his voice.

"This gig on tonight – is it members only, or can anyone rock up?"

"Very much open to anyone – that's the whole point of being 'evangelical'. That's the principle, although I do think there are a couple of people it doesn't sit very well with. They'd rather sing to their own choir."

"Less criticism or argument?"

I could hear his chuckle and nod down the phone line. "And for some, less prospect of 'bad influences' creeping in."

"Ah, that'd be me then. How can I resist that? What time, and where?"

So, that evening, I made my first appearance at a Christian Youth Fellowship event.

I was welcomed, cautiously. New faces weren't a common occurrence, whatever the evangelical aspirations. An almost complete absence of promotional effort had a lot to do with that, I reckon. They didn't do posters or handbills or anything like that. A one-line ad in the Classifieds under 'Religious Services' perhaps, if someone thought to place it, was the pinnacle of the advertising, and the words: "Youth Fellowship" plus an address and time, weren't exactly a clarion call to an audience.

While I waited in the foyer for Beeb, I looked inside the hall. It was simply laid out. A big bunch of flowers on the cupboard at the entrance. The cupboard held hymn books, spare Bibles for anyone who'd neglected to bring their own, and a few other accoutrements. The body of the hall was filled with a dozen rows of hard wooden bench seats – I didn't immediately think of them as 'pews' because of their complete lack of the ornamentation I associate with that word. Two aisles separated the seats into three phalanxes, and led to a modest stage, in front of which was a plain wooden lectern with a microphone fitted. A new organ sat off to one side. Apart from the flowers, the only decoration was a banner painted on the wall above the stage, reading "God is our refuge and strength".

Once Beeb appeared and we were visibly confirmed to be friends, the reception was a bit warmer. He'd obviously made an impression in the time he'd been part of their little community, and I could soon see why.

I couldn't call him 'charming', but he was unfailingly polite, listened attentively to people, smiled a lot, and didn't seem to look for arguments. Discussion, yes, but rather less willfully contrary than I'd known him to be.

"I don't want to argue with him," he quietly told me after a short conversation with an earnest, curly-haired young blonde man. "I just want him to *think*."

That was the challenge he'd set himself with many of the younger attendees of the Gospel Hall. Nearly all of them were at least second-generation members of the assembly, there because their family were already part of the flock and it was just expected and accepted that they would be too. There were four generations of one family I was later introduced to as 'regulars' (oddly enough, the seventy-something eldest of them the most open-minded, as it turned out). Beeb didn't object to anyone having a particular faith, but he believed it should be a considered choice, not an inheritance.

In that environment, the arrival of an 'outsider' with no existing family ties was something between a coup and a concern, particularly among some of the older cohort. When he said a lot of the right things, and presented himself well, and turned out to have a bit of charisma, he was at least accepted, and at best embraced. I don't think that had happened a lot in Beeb's experience so I reckon he was softening some aspects of his nature, perhaps even subconsciously, to foster that 'fitting in'. It struck me as a 'misfit' branch of the Christian religion, so it made sense for him to find a niche there.

The Youth Fellowship service itself was more entertaining than I expected. The first hour was a mixed bag of short speeches and/or Bible readings from mostly nervous teenagers and early twenties, musical acts (singers accompanied by guitar or piano), and communal singing. The music surprised and impressed me. Not conventional hymns, but something approaching 'folk-rock'. The lyrical content was appropriate to the setting, but it was upbeat, catchy – fun.

And then came the evening's 'guest speaker'. Up on to the stage at the front of the Hall strode Beeb, leaving me to share a pew – well, a bench – with Kelly Holden and his sister Anne, both quiet but good company.

He was good. No real surprise there for me. He opened with a smile and a nod of greeting to everyone, read a short poem that he'd penned for the occasion, then spoke off the cuff for half an hour. He started with Jesus' observation about "rendering unto Caesar that which is Caesar's" and extrapolated from there. He talked about being a part of the world, not apart from it. How can you change or improve things if you isolate yourself from them? How can you credibly communicate with people if you don't have anything to do with them? It wasn't "know your enemy", it was "understand your audience", and he deftly swung it around to cite Jesus' own life as the classic example of it. I was impressed.

He finished by inviting Anne Holden up to lead everyone in a closing prayer and song. It had been pre-arranged with her, but I do reckon it was Anne's first time in such a role – she had a blush you could have read by as she walked to the front of the hall. But she rose to the challenge. Sincerity trumped nervousness. Her quiet speaking voice turned into a singing voice not unlike Linda Ronstadt's, surprising but nice to listen to.

After 'the show' everyone gathered in a secondary building out the back of the assembly hall – the supper hall, it was called - for a good spread of sandwiches, scones, cakes and coffee. What my mother would have called a 'bunfight', but with no fighting.

I got introduced around, made appropriate polite noises, and even found myself getting involved in some interesting conversations with people who wanted to discuss Beeb's presentation. Some of the more intrinsically conservative ones, I'm sure reflecting the attitudes they'd grown up among, struggled with the idea of "opening oneself up to the corruption of the world".

"We have to be better than those people," one intense young bloke said to us.

The whole 'us and them' thing bothered me, but I tried to follow Beeb's diplomatic lead.

"Don't you have to know what it is you're being 'better' than?" I asked.

"Oh, I can see what they're like!" was the sharp reply.

"Seeing isn't the same as understanding. Why does someone behave in a particular way, do certain things…"

"Sin! It's all sin, and the work of the Devil!" snapped the young man, turning to snaffle another handful of cheesy crackers.

"Are all the gatherings like this?" I asked Beeb later.

"Youth Fellowships pretty much are. They happen one Saturday night per month, and on Sunday afternoons on alternate fortnights, usually at someone's house."

"A bit tricky to advertise those to a wider audience, I'd have thought."

"True enough," he agreed. "Very much a case of preaching to the converted, those afternoons. Though I did go to an open-air one on the beach – that was pretty effective."

"That makes a lot more sense if what you want to do is 'outreach', rather than stroke your own collective egos."

"I thought I was supposed to be the cynical one!" said Beeb with a laugh. "But you are right, Paddy. There is a tendency to be... introspective. That's not always a bad thing, but as you say, if the assembly wants to have a missionary role they have to make some effort to get out a bit. And the Sunday morning services do still feel like something of a closed shop. Oh, 'all welcome' is the statement, but the reality..."

"Only certain members of 'all' are welcome?"

"Let's say it's a little less inclusive than the Youth Fellowship."

I was already booked for that Sunday, but a week later I met up with Beeb at the Gospel Hall for the Sunday Service.

I'd made some effort to wear a 'respectable' outfit – a collared shirt and decent slacks as distinct from my usual jeans and t-shirt that even often passed as my regular work attire. But I was still conspicuously underdressed alongside a lot of folks who clearly took the term "Sunday best clothes" to heart. Lots of suits and collar-and-tie among the men, and nearly all of the women, whatever their age, in Good frocks - one step short of eveningwear, to my undiscerning eye.

What did strike me though, was that most of the women wore hats, or scarves or wraps on their heads. The ones who arrived without headgear collected a little piece of lace from the cupboard at the door, and draped it over their scalp.

"It's called a mantilla," Beeb explained. "Strange idea, that women can't attend the service bareheaded. Supposedly based on an instruction from the apostle Paul in Corinthians that hearkens back to man being created first. It's a very old-fashioned, 'orthodox' thing that I don't think serves them well."

"Seems a bit Catholic, or High Anglican to me," I agreed. I'd being doing a bit of research of my own. "I reckon some blokes perpetuate it out of fear of being distracted by a good-looking woman's hairstyle, whether that's conscious or not. There's a few things about this Paul bloke I wonder about."

Beeb nodded. "I'm inclined to agree. I thought the word was 'Christian', not 'Paulian' – I know whose teachings I prefer."

And there was the nub of what was to develop into his problem in the assembly. But that lay in the future. For now, he was becoming an accepted part of their community.

The Sunday service was structured on similar lines to what I'd experienced on the Saturday evening. The lectern had been relocated from in front of the stage to a loftier position up on it. The speakers tended to be older, the Bible readings longer, and the music more traditional. And in the middle of the service was what I thought of as the Communion, although that term wasn't used here – the passing around of a basket of dry biscuits and glasses of red wine (only possibly non-alcoholic, but certainly rough, from what I was told quietly by someone who knew). That 'breaking of bread' only extended to the first few rows of the hall, and as I noticed that, it occurred to me that there had been a discreet bit of 'ushering' to control who sat where. Not everyone in the assembly was equal, it seemed. The front rows were 'members only', like the Members' Stand at the cricket ground.

Nonetheless, I thought the service itself had a nice 'feel' to it. This morning's speakers, especially the main man, had a pleasantly pastoral air to them. More concern than condemnation, more care than criticism.

Over the next couple of months, I kept coming back. Not every week, but regularly. Some weeks, some 'sermons', were better than others. I found the speakers who stuck with the Gospels as their base much more digestible than others who worked from Paul's instructions, or worse, the Old Testament. A bad bout of 'thou shalt nots' would usually deter my return for a week or two.

There were some good people amongst the group. I immediately understood Beeb's regard for Kelly and his quiet sister. The MacAllisters were a genial and jovial family of Scots. Moose Mathers was a bloke about our age who was funny, self-deprecating and loved to laugh. And some likeable women, among them a particularly cute young lady named Janet.

She was eighteen or nineteen, but with such a slender figure you might not guess it. Her face had an almost pixie-like prettiness that made her age even harder to guess (and I suspect would continue to do so for years to come). Dark eyes, laughed readily, and loved music. I heard her sing one Sunday afternoon, something John Denver-esque as I recall. Not a great voice, even allowing for nerves, but an enthusiastic one.

Quite early in the piece, I realised Janet was flirting with me, and not being especially subtle about it. I was happy to respond in kind, but thought I'd better consult with Beeb on the 'local politics' before I decided to take things any further. I had a quiet word with him one Sunday morning before we went into the hall.

"Don't take her too seriously, mate," he advised. "She does that with every eligible young male she encounters I think."

"How to deflate an ego, old buddy. But thanks – suitably warned. The 'new kid in town' syndrome, you reckon?"

"Oh, not quite. She's flirted with me plenty of times, then gone off, then started again."

"Interesting environment to find a Bad Girl," I observed with a smile.

"I don't think she is."

"Ah. A Good Girl, who's experimenting?"

Beeb nodded. "More like it. She's got an older brother who's as imaginative as a stone, and a pair of ridiculously rigid parents whose collective imagination extends no further than fearing what Godless boys intend for their daughter. I think she's just reacting against them, to some extent. She is certainly a pretty flirt, I'll say that for her."

"Agreed. Shame about the family. They'll drive her in exactly the direction they don't want if they're not careful."

"Hmm, possibly. I think though, that at this stage Janet just doesn't really know *what* it is that she wants."

"Just like us, eh?"

He looked at me, not quite affronted. "Speak for yourself. I think I'm starting to know what it is that I want. The problem is in working out how to get it."

A crashing chord on the organ heralded the opening hymn, signalling that it was time for us stragglers to get into the hall and sit down.

Another thing that gradually dawned on me was the limited participation of the female members of the assembly. On rare occasions one might lead a hymn during a Sunday morning service, and I think once I heard a lady reading a few verses of Scripture. The Youth Fellowship meetings were a bit more egalitarian, but even that seemed a Work In Progress. Beeb's choice of Anne to close that first gathering I'd attended hadn't quite been 'shocking', but it was certainly unusual, and I'm sure that contributed to her nervousness at the time.

Before too long I even found myself moving out of being an observer, and becoming a participant. A couple of Bible readings (I got to pick my own verses, thank you very much), a five minute speech on Jesus' declaration of "the most important Commandments" and how I reckoned that should be the bottom line in 'following your faith' (love God with all your heart, soul and mind; and love your neighbour as much as yourself, in case the reference isn't familiar), even a little 'mini-revival' of Sky Blues one Saturday night.

We did two numbers. One was something I spun out of the 'love your neighbour/love one another' reference in Matthew's Gospel, playing up the character of the lawyer trying to entrap Jesus. The other was one of Beeb's poems that fitted well with the first, about seeking and seeing what was best in others, because that's where you'd find God. Went down well, too. I still remember the wide-eyed look on Janet's face when we came back to sit between her and the Holden siblings.

"Wow – I didn't know you could do that!" directed to both of us.

Both Beeb and I found ourselves starting to be drawn into the fabric of that Gospel Hall community. Our unusual position of not having an assembly 'pedigree' worked both for and against us. Neither expectations nor 'baggage'.

There was supposedly no formal hierarchy in the assembly. No priesthoods or ranks or ordained ministers. No central authority to whom everyone was even nominally answerable, except God, of course, but that was a bit nebulous and all too often open to interpretation. What there was, was 'leadership' by a group of Elders. Acknowledged, but not formalized. Powerful and dominant nonetheless. This same structure applied in all Gospel Halls, and as we visited them occasionally to enjoy their events like 'ours', I observed that the character of each community seemed ultimately driven by the characters of the dominant personalities among their Elders. Archly conservative, progressive, thoughtful, open-minded or hidebound.

Some of 'our' Elders had high hopes for us. Particularly for Beeb, who'd been around for a bit longer, was thus more of a known quantity, and frankly looked a bit more respectable than I did. I was rough around the edges, and getting rougher, although I did scrupulously keep my ever-increasing fondness for alcohol very Apart from my activities and presence at the Hall. I never once turned up drunk or hungover, although that is at least part of the explanation of why I wasn't around every week, either.

My old friend, though, seemed to offer something towards the growth and development of their little community, especially for those Elders who truly understood the concept of 'outreach'. They loved him as an articulate speaker who engaged the younger members of the flock – truthfully none of their second or third generation were much chop as speakers. Well, a couple of the girls were, but they didn't count. The boys and young men meant well, but that was as much as could be said. Janet's brother was earnest but deadly dull. Kelly's nervousness made his one-and-only attempt at public speaking almost inaudible, even with a microphone and amplifier turned up to full throttle. Moose was engaging, but somehow couldn't seem to be quite taken seriously.

To take the next step though, from 'guest speaker' at a Youth Fellowship to addressing the assembly on a Sunday morning, required a change in status. *We Are One In The Spirit, We Are One In The Lord* was a popular song among the assembly, but the reality was a little different. There was a distinction that was drawn.

It was the 'qualification' to sit in the front rows, and be offered a biscuit and a sip. One had to be baptized.

Baptism is a long-standing tradition in just about every branch or denomination of Christianity (and other religions). Jesus was baptized, and John the Baptist was one of the most significant figures in early Church history. But there's a big distinction made between 'infant baptism', which is pretty much what christening is, and baptism as a symbolic rite.

For those in the Gospel Hall, the ritual of baptism is a public declaration of faith. It won't get you into Heaven, so dunking a baby is entirely meaningless, not least because the infant hasn't made a conscious decision to have it done.

I think it was the patriarch of the MacAllister clan who was 'deputised' to quietly let Beeb know what the Elders had in mind, and nudge him along the way. And as Beeb related the conversation to me, it was all very polite and sincere and clearly well-intentioned.

I won't say "it got him thinking", because Beeb was thinking most of the time anyway, in my experience. However, Mister Mac's quiet words did prompt thoughts to travel in a particular direction. A week or two later he let it be known that yes, he'd like to be baptized, and was advised that "the Elders would see him" on the following Sunday, after the service.

This was the protocol. In effect, an interview with one or more of the leadership group, to approve the candidate's sincerity and ensure their understanding of the significance of the ceremony. Assuming that went well, one of the most senior Elders would be tasked with conducting the baptism as a part of a regular Sunday service – a 'special event extra', as it were.

There was a trapdoor in the stage at the front of the Hall. I'd noticed the recessed handle in the floor, but hadn't pursued the thought. It turned out that under that discreet bit of flooring was a rectangular tub – a bit bigger than a bath – with a couple of stairs built in for ease of entry and exit, and the necessary plumbing all hidden under the stage. All quite clever, really. That was where the performance was to take place.

Beeb surprised me by asking me to go to 'the interview' with him, surprising me more when he explained to me why. But I understood, approved, and appreciated what he wanted.

After the service concluded and most everyone had adjourned to the supper hall for the requisite tea and scones, three Elders remained behind. They rearranged one of the bench seats beside the right-hand aisle, swinging it around so that it faced the first row of the section that the bread and wine didn't get to. The symbolism was only a bit subtle, as they sat on the front pew looking back. Beeb was signalled to come over and join them.

Eyebrows were raised when I walked over as well, and sat down alongside him.

"I'd like Paddy to be with me for this," he explained.

There was a bit of "Er... well..." but it seemed there was nothing to suggest the applicant couldn't have the support of a friend, especially in the absence of a family member (who'd be the usual companion, if there was one).

The three-man panel – of course they were men, no woman got to be an Elder – happened to comprise three of the most 'venerable' members of the assembly. Not the oldest - one, Gawain Terence, was barely a decade older than Beeb and I – but the most conservative, although they'd probably have at least feigned shock to be described as such.

At their head was Barnaby Hoode. He was known amongst some of the younger regulars as 'Uncle Barney', but that was a less affectionate nickname than it sounded. Probably in his early fifties (I'm guessing by the ages of his two daughters, neither of whom came along early in his life) but looking older, he had one of the flimsiest avuncular acts I've ever encountered. It was as if someone had told him, "Barnaby, for the future of our Assembly, you *have* to foster good relations with our young people", and he'd reluctantly put up a façade whilst really waiting for everyone to 'catch up' and be as crusty, smug and grumpy as he was.

His patience was on its way to being rewarded in his younger daughter Lenore, whose 'people skills' could politely be described as confrontational. Older sister Jeanette was sweet-natured, rather shy, and totally overshadowed by her brassy sibling, alas.

The third member of the interview panel was Glenn Crowe, a generally affable used car salesman. He was one of nature's born followers, who left his initiative at the gate of the car yard whenever he walked out of work.

I'm not quite sure what Barnaby and his cohorts expected, or wanted, out of the interview. I suspect the intention was always to set the bar unusually high in terms of the commitments required of Beeb. But as it turned out, my presence was only the first curve that was thrown at them.

The early stages of the 'interview' went smoothly. Everyone was polite. Beeb gave cogent, well-considered answers to the questions put to him, and showed nothing but sincerity in his expressions of faith in Jesus. There might have been some 'points of order' that would be subject to later discussion – I know Beeb had already had some, let's say robust discussions with Gawain about questions of Biblical translation and interpretation, but nothing the panel could call irreconcilable differences.

Any reluctance on Hoode's part was camouflaged by his usual gruff manner as he said, "Alright, Mr. Bowmore. I think we can accept you into our Assembly. I'll conduct the ceremony in two Sundays time..."

"Ah, no," interrupted Beeb. "There's a Youth Fellowship outreach meeting at the beach next Saturday. I'd like to be baptized in the ocean, and I'd like Paddy to do it. If you'd like to be there and say a few words, of course that would be welcome."

If he'd announced that he'd arrived that morning by spaceship from Epsilon-6 he wouldn't have gotten a more dumbstruck reaction.

Judging by his expression, I think Glenn Crowe was about to say something along the lines of, "That seems okay," but Gawain jumped in first, while Barnaby was still spluttering.

"No, that's not how it's done. We have a way in which the service is always conducted," he stated.

"And it's conducted here! In the Hall!" Uncle Barney finally managed to say.

"Why is that?" Beeb asked mildly. "I can't find a specific reference in the Gospels. It seems that John baptized Jesus in the Jordan River. I'm showing a commitment to God, not just to the Gospel Hall."

"But the church, er, the Hall, is the body of God." This was not a conversation Hoode had ever had or rehearsed.

"I thought that's what Sunday's wafers represented?" I put in quietly, just adding slightly to the consternation.

"It's a building," Beeb said simply.

With something close to a 'harrumph' better suited to a man much older, Gawain said, "The Hall represents the Assembly. That's what you're being baptized into. Our community, the Children of God."

"We're all His children," Beeb replied. "All valued and valuable. All loved. That's why I want the ceremony to be on a public beach, not for an exclusive audience. And conducted by my best friend, who understands me and the statement I'm making, not by someone who's claiming some divine authority for the job."

There were a few moments of silence while the panel digested this. To me, it made perfect sense, and given the Assembly philosophy of the Bible as the guidebook for everything, I thought they didn't have much of a case to argue. Judging by the expressions on the faces of Hoode and Terence, I don't think they did either, and it burned them up.

Finally, Barnaby got his temper under some sort of control and through gritted teeth said, "Unless and until you can learn to respect authority, I don't think we can permit you to partake in the breaking of bread with us on Sundays."

Beeb nodded calmly. "I have the utmost respect for authority. The authority of what Jesus said and taught. If you can't respect that, then I think we have an insurmountable problem. You're concerned about the form of the ritual, I'm all about its meaning."

I threw my hat into the ring. "Frankly, it's the same with your wine and wafers. Jesus said 'remember me when you eat and drink', not 'go make a ritual out of it'. I have a communion with God every time I look at some part of His creation and go 'Wow!'. I don't need to be sitting with a select few on a Sunday to consider myself a Christian."

"Well said, old friend," responded Beeb, with a hand on my shoulder.

He stood up, clearly ending the interview before the panel could. I immediately did likewise. We smiled politely, and gave nods that were small bows. No hands were extended to be shaken, on either side. We walked out of the hall side by side.

I'd noticed Glenn Crowe nodding quietly as he considered what we'd said, but there was no sign of him saying anything. He wasn't about to stand up to Barnaby, or his heir apparent, but I suspected that Beeb had, again, met his objective of making at least one person think.

And who knows, if Crowe actually went on to talk with his family and others about what he'd just heard... Maybe there'd be some ripples in the pond.

"Did you want to go out the back for coffee and final farewells?" I asked, sensing correctly that there'd just been a parting of the ways with the Gospel Hall.

He paused, thinking. "One or two people, yes. I don't think it'll take long."

We were having a quiet chat with Moose, Janet and the Holdens when the panel came into the supper hall and were immediately joined by their coterie. We'd deliberately been vague and evasive about the conduct of the interview, trying to be tactful despite both feeling that such diplomacy seemed scarcely deserved.

Then Lenore Hoode stormed over to stand near us. Hands on hips, she glared at Beeb, ignoring the rest of us as though we were passing ants.

"I heard how you disrespected my father. God will *get* you for that!" she snapped, then turned on her toes and marched away again.

I don't think I was the only one who stood open-mouthed at the heart-felt viciousness in that outburst.

"What was that all about?" Moose asked.

"Ah, you know what she's like," replied Janet, surprisingly dismissive. A healthy attitude, I thought.

"Time we left?" Beeb asked me softly.

"Reckon so. My name's Paddy, not Martin Luther. I'm not here to create a schism."

A momentary look of intrigue, temptation even, crossed my old mate's face, but he nodded agreement. We gave hugs all around the little group we were with, and wished them well, then departed, leaving them puzzled and perturbed.

Neither of us went back to the Gospel Hall. The Assembly's loss, as far as I was concerned, although I was sure at least some of the 'leadership group' wouldn't agree. Not everyone likes being challenged to think, or appreciates having their followers so challenged. I had a hunch the 'outreach program' wasn't going to get very far, in the immediate future at least.

I didn't pursue any alternative religious options. My faith was my own, and I was content with it. Probably a bit stronger and better 'educated' for my time at the Hall, but reassured that I didn't need a dedicated building to support it, far less a formal institution. I think Beeb was much the same. I can't say he was disillusioned about the internal politics, because I don't reckon he was under any illusions in the first place.

Whatever faith he'd been willing to publicly proclaim by my baptizing him remained internalized. He never raised the matter again, and I never prompted it. And without the regular meet-ups at the Hall, we saw each other less often, amicably drifting back into our own paths.

There's a sad postscript to this story, unfortunately. Some months later I happened to meet Janet in a coffee shop in town. She told me that she'd cut her ties to the assembly to the point of leaving home.

When I jokingly said something like, "Not because of me, or Beeb, I hope," she shook her pretty head firmly.

Bitterness in her voice, she explained why. Kelly Holden had become aware of some definite Feelings towards another young bloke. It was never made clear who. Maybe it *was* Beeb, or me, Moose, or even Janet's brother (although that's hard to imagine). But Kel was troubled. Not so much by the feelings themselves, but how to reconcile them with the community that he'd only recently been at last baptized into.

Instinctively he knew better than to seek guidance from the Elders, despite their theoretically pastoral role, and while he'd discussed it with Anne, he wanted a 'second opinion' from someone he trusted. Janet was his best friend, he'd said, and talked with her quietly one Sunday morning in the supper hall.

Not quietly enough, apparently. Lenore Hoode had overheard, if not the whole conversation, enough to go scurrying to her father.

The following Sunday morning Gawain Terence had chosen a particularly fire-and-brimstone reading from the Old Testament about the punishments due to a man who coveteth another man (along with several other Major Sins). Then, following that up, Barnaby Hoode delivered the morning's main sermon. More fire, more brimstone, more eternal damnation. And in the course of it, a very public naming and shaming of Kelly Holden in front of a shocked assembly.

Kelly's immediate response was to maintain a quiet dignity. Despite the two Elders' efforts, he didn't express any humiliation. No denial, not even remorse, only a comment of having 'something to think about'. He didn't stay for the bunfight afterwards, obviously. There was apparently a clear division between those who wanted to support him in some way, whether they sympathized with his alleged 'unforgiveable lifestyle choice' or not, and those who wouldn't be seen to stand anywhere near him. But before he and Anne left, Kelly made a point of saying to anyone within earshot that his belief was in a God of Love, not Vengeance.

It turned out though that Kelly was far more fragile than anyone realised – the day after this public pillorying, he took a massive overdose of his mother's sleeping pills.

Anne never returned to the Gospel Hall. Uncle Barney apparently never apologised, Janet told me grimly. Instead, he, and especially Lenore, claimed it as vindication. "Only a guilty soul would do that."

Her own family had taken the Hoodes' side, citing Barnaby as 'a good man'. Janet had packed her bags that night, found a flat, and was waiting for a transfer interstate.

So much for 'we are one in the Spirit', I thought.

13

BROTHEL

I've been described before as a 'serial monogamist', and I've got no objections to that. Unfortunately for my deep-down happiness, I was between relationships, and had been for some time. Even casual flings weren't happening for me.

Mostly I told myself it didn't bother me, and had another drink. Probably that was a big part of the problem, but I hadn't figured that out yet.

What I had figured out was that I was still driven by hormones, peaking and troughing in a cycle we used to call biorhythms. It's not that I only thought about sex for a few days a month. The *thought* was pretty much constant, allowing for distractions of food, music, sport, even work. Spike Milligan once observed that the only way bromide could stop a British soldier from thinking about sex would be if you loaded it into an artillery shell and fired it point blank into his crotch. I understood. But sometimes the feeling was stronger than mere thought. Call it longing.

Porno magazines and movies, and the self-gratification that came with them, were okay up to a point. For some guys I think they were better than 'the real thing' – no conversation, no awkward foreplay, no risk of any emotional involvement. But for me, all those things were part and parcel of enjoying sex. Even so, at those peak times what I really craved was human touch. Someone else's touch, I mean.

Experience, at University and beyond, had taught me I wasn't good at one-night-stands, or brief flings. I never mastered 'pick-up' lines. (I was often bemused by what worked for other blokes. I knew one who had astonishing success with, "Do you like chicken? Cos I've got something here that's fowl...") I was under no illusions about my attractiveness, except possibly to have a lower opinion of it than at least some girls and women I'd known. Sometimes I made inappropriate choices, pursuing, or at least lusting after, the unattainable.

And more than once I read too much into a relationship. At least two of the Janes should only ever had been friends, or at best, friends with benefits. They were always going to be more than 'quick'n'dirty' – none of us were that way inclined. But hopelessly romantic Paddy got smitten and sought something more than the ladies really expected or wanted. Fun while it lasted, but done too soon.

One spring evening when I was feeling particularly frustrated and lonely, as I flicked through the newspaper I noticed an ad. I'd doubtless seen it many times before, but never paid it any particular attention. It was for a 'Gentleman's Club' in Spring Hill. A silhouette of a long-legged girl was less eye-catching for me than the words *Our ladies can be just what you need.*

It would be quite a few years before a fine band called The Whitlams would have their biggest hit single, but their lyric *"there's no aphrodisiac like loneliness"* was true long before they wrote it down and recorded it.

Suddenly I had a very clear idea of 'just what I needed'.

Spring Hill wasn't a long drive away. Certainly not long enough for me to have any second thoughts beyond 'there's a first time for everything'.

I know prostitution is disapproved of by many, notwithstanding it sometimes being called 'the oldest profession'. But I reckon it's a considerably lesser evil than other options. Transactional sex is a better option than getting satisfaction by force – domestically or imposed on some undeserving unwilling stranger.

That was the gist of the conversation going on inside my head as I drove. Maybe it was self-justification, but by the time I walked into the Club I felt like I was making the right choice.

The small entrance foyer was attended (guarded?) by a bloke who was clearly of Pacific Island origin. He was tall and broad, probably one-and-a-half times my weight, and not much of that was fat. His bulk made the counter he sat behind look almost absurdly tiny. If he wanted to get out from behind it in a hurry it would collapse like a paper bag full of ice cubes.

His response to my arrival was to look me up and down once, nod, grunt, "Evenin' mate," and jerk a thumb to indicate I should go through the heavy red curtain on his right.

That took me into a bar. Big enough for a couple of stools, one occupied by a bloke sitting with his back to the entrance, and around the walls two couches and a couple of armchairs. The lighting was dim, for both mood and privacy. A television mounted on the wall was displaying a porn video. The picture quality was grainy and the sound was off, so it wasn't much of a distraction. Much easier on the ear than the grunts and groans would have been, recorded guitar music played quietly through discreet speakers. Django Reinhardt was the musician, I noticed, approving of someone's taste in jazz.

As my eyes adjusted to the low illumination, I realised that there was a small middle-aged woman behind the bar, polishing glassware.

"What'll you have, love?" she asked me in a voice that had come from a sheep station somewhere out west. It seemed an odd question in this establishment, then I realised she was referring to a drink.

"Vodka and tonic. Thanks," I replied.

The figure on the stool near me gave a start and turned around.

"Hello Paddy," said Beeb as casually as if this was a bar we met in every week.

"G'day mate," I replied, resisting the momentary urge to ask 'what are you doing here?', which would have been a bloody silly question. I determined to be as casual as my old friend.

"First drink's on the house," said the woman I immediately took to be in charge. "Especially for polite customers!" she added with a broad smile.

With a soft sigh Beeb said, "That explains why Vic paid for his round."

"The one with eyebrows like caterpillars?" asked the barmaid, not bothering to hide a sneer.

Beeb nodded, somehow implying apology in the movement.

"Vic?" I asked.

Unbidden, Beeb related the story of how he'd come to be there. A young bloke who worked in the same department, Winston Uxbridge by name, was soon to be married. Over lunch that day he'd made a remark about 'lacking experience with a woman'. Some of his colleagues decided that this would never do, and it would be a generous gesture, and an act of kindness to both Winston and his future bride, to remedy the shortfall in the lad's education. Office barfly and would-be Lothario Vic O'Neill knew 'just the place'.

Word went around the male population in and around the area where Beeb worked that an expedition to the Gentleman's Club was planned for the evening, with a whip-round to be arranged to pay for young Winston's education. More than one person wondered aloud the incongruity of O'Neill having any connection with the word 'Gentleman'. He used toilets with the word written on the door, but that was as close as he was known to come. Besides Vic, two other blokes expressed interest in the adventure: Bob Halloran and Dave Knight. Beeb was trying to make an effort to engage socially with some of his co-workers. After willingly 'chipping in' to the appeal for donations, he had realised that the whole project had him intrigued. So, to the surprise of the other four, he'd accompanied them to the Club.

Vic had tried to swagger past the man-mountain at the front door like he owned the place, and very nearly got them all barred from entry. The diplomatic skills of Halloran and Beeb had managed to resolve the problem. Beeb in fact had stopped to converse with the bouncer, interested in the man's personal history. While he'd been learning of Sualesi's ambitions to play international rugby, his four colleagues had gone inside and ordered drinks. By the time he caught up, O'Neill was pocketing his change (and grumbling about the prices) just as four girls entered the bar from a green door in the corner.

In a scene that he admitted had overtones of a meat market, the blokes had selected a girl each. The penalty for being last in was that Beeb would have to wait ten minutes or so, for some new girls whose shift was just about to start. He didn't mind, content to sit quietly at the bar and take in his surroundings. As Guest of Honour, Winston was given first choice. Beeb wondered if his other companions had noticed the very discreet moment of familiarity between the young man and the blonde he'd chosen. Probably not, distracted by making their own selections.

The barmaid was the soul of discretion, of course, but Beeb fancied he saw a flash of wry amusement when, left alone at the bar, he'd explained to her the story of their visit. He was quite sure that Winston's convincing act of naivety was just that – a convincing act. Never mind, it wasn't like he'd invested heavily in the fellow's "education", and he wasn't likely to encounter the soon-to-be Mrs. Uxbridge.

Beeb's tale had taken a little while to tell, delayed further by my laughter and occasional questions. Delicately, he then enquired about what had brought me to the Club, presuming correctly that I was again unattached.

"Still looking for The One?"

"Not looking, as such, but open to the possibility of finding her. Meanwhile..."

"Yes. Meanwhile. I understand."

I'm not sure quite what I'd have replied if he'd pursued the question further, when the barmaid put down the handset of what was evidently an internal phone system.

"Here you are, gents. Your ladies have arrived," she said breezily.

Through the green door stepped two very attractive young women. Both had long hair, slim figures, and were barely the height of the tip of my nose, but that was where the resemblance to each other ended. One was blue-eyed and blonde, with light eyebrows that suggested that the colour was achieved without chemical assistance.

The other girl was Asian, with eyes almost as dark as her sleek black hair.

"Patience has its own rewards, Paddy," said my companion quietly, by which I understood that the ladies available to us were rather more attractive than those servicing his four colleagues who'd had first pick.

The blonde grinned widely and said, "Hi! I'm Alice."

"Hello, I am Suzie," said the dark girl, with a small bow and a more demure smile.

I rested a hand on Beeb's shoulder and said, "First come, first served, old pal."

"Thank you. Shall we catch up... afterwards?"

We quickly agreed to meet in a bar a few minutes' walk away and set a time for it, shaking hands on the arrangement. We each quietly handed the appropriate fee over the bar, where it immediately vanished below the counter, not into the bar till. Then he walked to the girls, bowed chivalrously to both, and extended a hand to the blonde.

"Good evening, Alice," he said.

"Good choice! Let her take you to Wonderland," called the barmaid cheerfully.

I was a little surprised at Beeb's choice. Asian girls were still 'exotic' back then, not flooding the market like now, if you believe the on-line ads. If that particular aspect of international trafficking in human flesh had reached Australia, it was only just establishing its roots. White girls, white women, were still in the majority in the sex trade. Oh, I understood that there were some half-castes and ladies of 'mixed race', but I heard that they were more common out in the country. It was the only work many of them could get, but that was just as true for a lot of the Caucasian women in the business, both in the city and in regional areas.

I think he just willed himself not to go for the 'other' in this instance, and wondered if he saw in Suzie an echo of Priti, for all that she was of a very different race. Despite the passage of time, I suspected that wound was still tender if poked unexpectedly or injudiciously.

Being 'left with' Suzie was no hardship for me. I had pretty much zero experience with Asian women at that point. The few I'd known at Uni seemed to keep to themselves in their own little cliques, and the local community I covered for my newspaper was almost exclusively Anglo-Saxon, with a smattering of Mediterranean. But she was quite lovely, and I admit I was intrigued.

I took Suzie's hand and gave a respectful bow, which seemed to momentarily surprise her, before she led me out the green door and up some stairs to a long corridor. The third door on the left led into what was evidently 'her' room.

As unfamiliar as I was to this particular situation, I quickly realised that my consort for the next hour didn't have a great deal more experience. And such that she had, didn't seem to have been especially positive. She seemed genuinely surprised that the first thing I wanted to do with her was chat. Almost bewildered that I might be interested in her, not just sex.

She's been still in the process of disrobing when I started to talk to her. She'd shucked the low-cut white satin top, and was reaching back to fumble with the clasps of her lacy red bra when I laid my hand on hers.

"Don't rush. There's no hurry," I said.

Her momentarily raised eyebrows were my first clue that her time in the job had been neither long nor particularly happy. I stood behind her and unfastened the tiny hooks, then ran my hands through her hair. It was like strands of silk. I leaned forward and kissed the back of her head before she turned to face me and removed the t-shirt I was wearing.

As she ran her hands over my chest I tilted her head up to make the eye contact she'd tried to subtly avoid. I smiled as warmly and honestly as I could, hoping to put her more at ease.

"It's not really 'Suzie', is it?" I asked. "I really hope you weren't named for the old film *The World Of Suzie Wong.*"

That got me a blank look. "1960. William Holden. Romantic movie set in Hong Kong," I explained.

The blank look lifted only slightly, but she did smile coyly and quietly say, "Zuanshi."

"Ah, I see where 'Suzie' comes from. Zuanshi is pretty. It suits you."

I won't go into details of what happened next. It was fun, and I did my best to make sure that was true for both of us. Zuanshi was certainly responsive enough for me to believe she was enjoying herself. I was pleased she wasn't the hurrying, 'wham, bam, thank-you ma'am' type, but I was (hopefully we were) thoroughly satisfied well before the hour was up. It allowed the two of us to lie together in comfortable afterglow for a little while.

She stroked the beard I was still cultivating, and looked me in the eye, which I sensed wasn't something she often did with a client. Her English wasn't great, but adequate. Her voice was soft.

"You very gentle man," said Zuanshi in something just above a murmur.

"Is that unusual?" I asked.

There was sadness in her voice as she answered, "Sometimes, yes."

"That's ironic, in a Gentle-man's Club."

The pun was lost on Zuanshi. "Even kind looking men, sometime they come here, they behave different."

I thought about that, pleased that I didn't seem to be being included in that lamentable category. "Like they have an opportunity, an excuse even, to be the tough guy."

"Tough guy?"

"Behave like a bad man, in ways that they never otherwise do."

"Bad man, yes. Too many bad men."

I wondered if some of that behaviour was a product of her race. The anti-Asian sentiment that had flourished in Australia post-World War 2 was still quite strong. Less suppressed than it is now, when politeness, political correctness, tourism dollars and the weight of immigrant numbers all combine to dissuade people from giving voice to attitudes that still run deep.

My suspicion, though, was that all of the girls were vulnerable to abuse. The nature of the job gave them the status of rented property, and there are plenty of hire cars, tools and equipment, even houses and flats, that are testimony to how poorly, badly some people treat things they use that aren't their own.

Zuanshi evidently read my concerned expression. She stroked my face and said, "Not worry too much. If trouble get bad, there is button I can press, low down beside bed, call for help."

"The big bloke on the front desk?" I asked. "Well, he's big enough to sort out trouble, that's for sure."

"Oh, Sualesi?" The girl laughed. "He useless! Too big and slow, and not supposed to leave front door anyway."

Suddenly it clicked for me who the real 'enforcer' would be. The barmaid-manager, who I realised was as tough as nails and probably had that deceptive wiry strength of so many folks born and raised in the country. I could imagine her looking, and being, suitably threatening, with or without any sort of weapon in her hands.

"He a good man, though," Zuanshi continued. "Speak nice to us all, and not expect free-bees from girls like man before him."

I didn't suppose that a lot of the blokes in Sualesi's profession were paragons of virtue – certainly some of the Security Staff I'd encountered were little more than thugs getting paid for nastiness and bullying they'd otherwise have done as a hobby. It was reassuring to hear that they weren't all like that. And particularly so to find that this one, while of limited value as 'protection', at least wasn't adding to the occupational hazards of someone I genuinely liked.

We snuggled comfortably together for a little while longer. She told me a little of her home in Taiwan, left behind in the hope of earning the decent money she'd never make there without a better education, apparently. I told her about places in Australia that I'd visited. Her eyes shone at descriptions of the Great Barrier Reef. All too soon a discreet little alarm pinged softly.

"Time you must go," said Zuanshi, softening the announcement with a gentle kiss.

We rolled off the bed and pulled our clothes back on, reluctantly in my case. At the door of her room Zuanshi stopped, put her arms around me and hugged.

"Thank you," she said, a nanosecond before I said exactly the same thing.

We held the embrace for a moment. If she wasn't a damn fine actress, she'd found the last hour more enjoyable than many in her working life. That boosted my ego, but also made me happy for her sake. The hopeless romantic in me was stirring already.

A month or so later I phoned the Club and asked to make a booking for an hour with Zuanshi. "Suzie," I corrected myself. The voice on the other end of the line – not the bar manager I'd met, I was sure of that – told me she didn't work there now. But there were other girls who would be able to satisfy me, certainly. I said, "No thanks," and hung up, surprised at the level of my disappointment. I just hoped she'd found a situation that kept her safe and happy, wherever that might be, in Australia or back in Taiwan. Maybe she'd made her way up to the reef and had a good job there. I liked that thought.

But that was still in the future. This night I made my way out the side door of the Club that was reserved for departing clients. Maybe management didn't want us comparing notes with new arrivals.

It didn't take me long to get to the bar where Beeb was already waiting for me. His drink was still barely touched so I figured he'd not beaten me there by much. We chatted briefly about our respective workplaces, but it wasn't a subject either of us had any enthusiasm for. Inevitably we turned to the experience we'd just had. Not intrusively, but with the curiosity we'd shared for as long as we'd known each other.

I told him what I knew about Zuanshi, which admittedly wasn't much, but just enough to be interesting. I wondered whether he thought maybe he'd made the wrong choice, but he explained that Alice had proved interesting in her own ways.

When he'd been taken into her room, Beeb realised that he really wanted a conversation at least as much, if not more, than sex. It seemed that wasn't a new experience for the girl, although at first, she was a little concerned.

She'd asked, "Don't you fancy me, after all? Or is something the matter with you? We do get blokes with... problems. Often I can help, if you want?"

"Thanks," he replied. "But it's not about me – it's about us."

"What 'us'?"

"Exactly. I know that for a certain amount of money I'll get a certain amount of pleasure from you. You may or may not get any pleasure from me, and that's my point. If you're a good actress, I'd never know."

"So, if I'm good, you go away happy, right?"

"Um – yes – I guess so."

"Well then, isn't *that* the point? My job is to make you feel special. The more dollars you pay, the more special I make you."

Beeb smiled – he liked Alice. "Who makes you feel special?" he asked.

"Me?" It was as though the question had never been asked before.

"Yes. You. When do *you* get to be the one who is made special?"

"Ah!" She gave a small, but genuine laugh. "That happens outside working hours."

"That doesn't say much about job satisfaction."

Another laugh. "Oh honey – I'm not in this business for job satisfaction! You're a nice bloke, so I'll be honest with you. It's a way to pay the bills, and keep me and my little girl fed. That's not to say I don't enjoy it , sometimes at least, but it's not why I'm here." Correctly reading the interested expression on her client's face she continued. "It's different for different girls. We talk, y'know. Look out for each other as best we can. For some, each other's company is the best part of the job. Mostly it's about the money – for family, for drugs, paying for study. One girl saves up for an overseas trip every year. But I've known a couple who got into it just 'cos they really, really like sex. Good luck to them, I say. Get paid for doing what you enjoy. I mean, I enjoy it when it's good, but it isn't why I'm here. So... why are *you* here?"

Beeb laughed in appreciation of having his curiosity reflected back at him. Alice was good at more than the physical aspects of her job.

"Support for a fellow I work with. Intellectual curiosity, I suppose. And yes, a degree of physical loneliness, if I'm honest with myself."

And with a smile, Alice proceeded to address that particular issue. Very effectively, Beeb admitted.

"Not a long-term solution, obviously, but certainly fun while it lasted."

I nodded. Both of us were smiling, but I think neither of us wore expressions of true delight. Satisfaction maybe, but more than a hint of wistfulness or something like it. I know that, as much as I'd enjoyed Zuanshi's services, there was a definite sense of incompleteness. For all that Beeb was less emotionally driven than I was (mostly), I had a hunch he was feeling something similar. We'd had fun, and learned a bit, including about ourselves, but our underlying situations hadn't changed.

"Well, that's some hormonal pressure relieved, anyway. Not so much emotional, alas, but that's to be expected when you think about it," I said.

Raising his glass in agreement Beeb added, "A place like that is a monument to loneliness, for both the patrons and the staff."

"Some of them, anyway," I demurred. "From what your girl said, there's a sort of camaraderie amongst them, at least."

"Mm... I suspect it's the camaraderie of the occupants of a lifeboat. Shared trauma, rather than true companionship."

At the risk of giving too much credit to the people running the Gentlemen's Club and places like it, perhaps that's why they don't make it easy for the clients to get together 'after the event'. Not just to avoid comparisons between the girls, that might deter repeat custom rather than encourage it. But to reduce the risk of taking the 'gloss' off the experience with too much shared introspection. Mind you, in my experience, a lot of us blokes don't tend to go deep in conversations.

We'll talk shoulder to shoulder, rather than eye to eye, and give as little away emotionally as possible.

It had always been one of the things that made Beeb different, and our friendship unusual – a willingness to go beyond the obvious topics of conversation and explore under the surface. Not often, especially in the latter couple of years, but I realised that there was a level of trust there that didn't have to be stated. It just *was*. I know there was nobody else in my life I'd have talked to about feeling emotionally isolated, and I believe it was the same for him.

Ironic, then, that we didn't ever acknowledge that our friendship was so important in addressing that very isolation.

Not that there was ever any hint or suggestion of physicality between us. Like many an adolescent male we'd both had some curiosity about homosexuality. Just not with each other. Most teenagers are potentially bisexual, I reckon, even though a lot (of any gender) don't admit it, even to themselves. Decisions should get made based on experience and (suitably careful) experiment, but peer and parental pressure are all too often in the way. I don't think Beeb ever pursued the question very far, but then, after Priti he didn't pursue any relationship very far. I'd explored a couple of times, but simply found girls more satisfying, especially emotionally.

And that was the shortcoming of the Gentlemen's Club, I'm afraid.

Only a really misguided or delusional bloke would go to a brothel to find a real Relationship. But for some of us, sex without a suggestion of romance is an unattractive thing. Like imagining Botticelli's *Venus* with a crew cut. The 'missing bit' only assumes more importance.

Sometimes the efforts we make to overcome loneliness only serve to emphasise it.

⌇

14

BOOZE

Beeb and I were having one of our all-too-infrequent catch-ups. A few rounds of convivial drinks and chat, Saturday lunchtime. Our venue was the Queen Street Bar of the "New" York Hotel, very particularly chosen as we were acutely aware of the rapid decline in the number of historic pubs in Brisbane over the previous few years, and we knew it was earmarked for destruction soon. All but the façade, like others to be 'maintained' as frontage to the shopping monolith that was to dominate the already heritage-carnivorous Queen Street Mall.

We'd hoped, or at least I'd hoped (Beeb was politely agreeable) to be joined by our old friend Eric 'Fish' Jones. 'A fish could only aspire to drink like Eric Jones', was a popular phrase of earlier times. But our world was changing. Fish had gotten his medical degree, a placement in a hospital while he contemplated his own practice, and a new partner, a recently graduated nurse named Penny.

Like the rest of our little gang, I'd tried to like Penny. It wasn't mutual. As far as she was concerned we, collectively and individually, were a bad influence on him. There was doubtless some truth in that, and in the similar observation that sometimes Fish was a bad influence on us – I know I tried matching him drink for drink on a few, memorably messy occasions. But I and we saw less and less of our old drinking buddy as he worked on taking his profession, and his relationship, more seriously. I think the latter was very much the source of impetus, let's politely say encouragement, for the former.

"I think, like a few student nurses we met, she had an agenda of hooking up with a doctor at earliest opportunity. Call me cynical, but it seems a more comfortable long term option than a career of needles, bodily fluids, bedpans and a bad back from lifting dead weights."

"Yes, Paddy, you're cynical. That doesn't mean I disagree with you. Not all of them of course, far from it. But I can think of a couple we met," Beeb agreed. "I can recall all too clearly Penny leading Fish away from a party by the arm, telling him he should come home and forget about 'the riff-raff', as she put it."

"Yeah, I heard that expression used a few times, too. Tried laughing it off as a *Rocky Horror Picture Show* reference..."

"Well, yes, you did lead quite a few Richard O'Brien singalongs as I recall."

"It's just a jump to the left..."

We laughed at the shared memory of a crowded table in the Refectory, all singing or shouting, "But it's the pelvic thrust that really drives you insa-a-a-ane, let's do the Time Warp again!" before tumbling off our chairs in happy homage to a favourite scene.

"Now *there* is a classic movie" I said.

"Certainly, a memorable one," Beeb agreed.

We ordered more drinks. Bourbon and soda for Beeb, vodka and tonic for me.

"I've developed a taste for these on pub crawls," I observed. "Only slightly more expensive these days, and a healthier option than beer, I found."

Beeb raised his eyebrows. "Healthy?"

"Clear fluid," I explained. "Too many schooners and I tended to wobble like a zeppelin. Far fewer calories than beer." I patted a tummy that, while not trim, was less flabby than I probably deserved.

"Mm. Interesting theory. I stick to bourbon for the taste," he said.

"Oh, speaking of pub crawls – thanks for the invitations to the annual event. I've been tempted, but, well, it's not the drinking – I'm just not comfortable with crowds any more."

"No worries. Mind you, I don't think we've yet drawn a 'crowd'. I think we've peaked at eight."

"That's rather a shame, given the occasion. Now you make me think I really *should* join in."

"That'd be good, even if only for a bar or two, raise a couple of glasses to the memories," I nodded.

The 'annual event' we were talking about was a memorial pub crawl in honour of the old Belle Vue Hotel. The heritage-listed pub, boasting Brisbane's finest accommodation in times past, temporary home to Katherine Hepburn, Ava Gardner, the Queen Mother and touring cricket teams among other luminaries, had been located inconveniently for a State Government who wanted to expand their office-tower fiefdom. The grand old building had been bought by them, stripped of its famous wrought ironwork, and allowed to fall into rapid decline.

Then, one April midnight in 1979, they'd had it demolished. The late hour was in the hope of avoiding the media and protestors regularly on site, who'd been waiting for just such an act of vandalism. It didn't work. There was still much ruckus and several arrests, and strong words in the press – even the archly conservative *Courier-Mail* expressed concern at the way the deed had been done.

There was some comfort gained from the City Council blocking plans for a new office building for years. A shadeless, soulless garden and a statue of a scowling Queen Elizabeth II marked the old Belle Vue site for quite a while, before one more glass and chrome box was finally erected. (That has since been demolished, too, presumably to make way for another like it.)

The Belle Vue wasn't the first historic old pub to fall, but the manner of her demise made her a bit more iconic. A suitable rallying point for an annual event to remember those places being lost in a depressingly regular succession. We made our way from bar to bar around the CBD, raising our glasses to history. I know it sounds like an excuse, but for most of those attending, in those early days especially, we were sincere.

Beeb would have been a good fit, a fact he'd perhaps just come to appreciate. Our conversation turned to the changing face of Brisbane's streetscape.

The beautiful stained-glass peacock windows of the Railway Hotel, demolished to make way for the appropriately ugly new police headquarters. The Wintergarden, gone in '81, one of the first to make way for the Mall. She'd been followed by Her Majesty's. There had been great promises about her unique façade being saved – the carved faces of Will Shakespeare and other literary notables gazing down benignly on the drinkers as they entered and exited HM's lavish bar. It didn't happen. Perhaps the bloke behind the wrecking ball didn't get the memo. Or perhaps the developers didn't really care.

As the Mall crept south towards the river, and the great shopping block was planned, more went. The Carlton. The Arcadia on Elizabeth Street, which had backed onto the new site – once home to a beer garden at the rear where an after-work drink could be enjoyed by starlight, nestled among brick walls and potted plants. The York, whose remains we currently sat in. The Queen Street Bar was little more than a brightly lit tunnel, with bar and taps on the left as you walked in, stools and a few cramped booths on the right. The nightclub downstairs had more dark ambience, furnished in part with a few barrels that had been in the mostly-demolished York before it was given the New pronoun.

As we both observed, though, it wasn't just the pubs that were being wrecked, and missed. Trades Hall had been closed, and was scheduled to soon 'make way' for some corporate headquarters. The deconsecrated but still lovely old church that had become the Scaramouche, arguably the best French restaurant Brisbane ever had. We mourned the loss of the admittedly non-descript building that had housed the Alouette, the dingy but character-laden little downstairs coffee lounge where Beeb and I had enjoyed many an evening of jasmine tea and Sobranjes.

And of course, Cloudland, the ballroom that had sat for decades on the Bowen Hills skyline before another late-night demolition job in 1982. Its superbly sprung dance floor and elegant eggshell fragment of a front porch were etched in the minds of patrons of countless musical gigs. It had been home to pre-, mid- and post-war dances that lifted weary spirits, and been the venue for many school formals and dances for those educational institutions which, unlike our wealthy establishment, couldn't afford to build or maintain their own suitably sized hall.

"Hark at us," I said sadly after another vodka. "Barely mid-twenties, and already pining for past glories. And not even our own."

"Mm. *The* past, not our past. And just elements of that. Buildings, places."

"Icons, though. Cultural icons. And the loss of that culture they represented – that's what I'm lamenting. The art and the beauty of HM's, and the Railway's window."

"Oh, I see your point, Paddy. And as well as losing the art itself we seem to have lost the appreciation of it. We collectively, I mean. Not we individually."

He gave a sympathetic pat on my non-drinking arm.

"Of course. I mean, there's grieving for memories. Great gigs I saw at Cloudland. Great nights at the Queens, even the Belfast. Drinks at the Grosvenor, before it became a bloody MacDonalds. Probably in any or all of them a few missed opportunities too, of one sort or another..."

A few attractive faces danced across my mind as I looked into my glass.

"But also grieving for never having the opportunity to *see* those particular beautiful things again," I continued.

"Too many people had already stopped seeing what was there, old friend. That's what happened. Who looks up and admires the scenery as they walk along a city street any more?"

"Maybe that's why I drink," I mused. "Dull the pain of that grieving for what I – we – have lost."

There was the silence of drinks being thoughtfully consumed before Beeb responded, "Plausible, Paddy. You wouldn't be the first, and I'm sure not the last, to anaesthetize things that went before. The pain of the bad and the loss of the good. Drink to forget, until you've forgotten what or why."

Something dispassionate in his voice impinged on my vodka-impaired brain. It wasn't condescending, but neutral.

"Not the case for you, then?" I asked, trying not to be irked by the lack of enthusiastic agreement I'd anticipated (stupidly, or at least drunkenly, if I'd really considered my companion's long-established nature).

The last of the latest glass of bourbon was swallowed at a gulp, and he gestured to the barman for a refill, actions I promptly duplicated.

After some time, he replied, "No. I still appreciate the past, but it doesn't pain me. It's done. I don't want to wallow in it – no offence, I'm not saying that's what you're doing."

He was diplomatic, but probably closer to the truth than a sober me would have liked.

We were talking shoulder to shoulder, not eye to eye. That's a bloke thing – women apparently look at each other's faces when they have Serious Conversations, but most males find that really uncomfortable. Side by side lends itself more readily to long thoughtful silences, and we were both deep in our own reveries.

I've heard it said that alcohol is a depressant. I'm no doctor, but in my observation that isn't true. It's a mood amplifier. If you're in a good mood, you're likely to get happier and more boisterous as you get drunk, and liable to do stupid things. If you're feeling down, you'll probably get more miserable or angry as you get drunk, and liable to do stupid things.

It's a good servant, but a lousy master. Drinking had steadily become a problem for me over the years. It had been the wedge that drove Writer Jane and I apart, although I took a while to realise it. Likewise, it was only in hindsight that I was aware of the problems it had caused between Angela and I.

While I was pondering past relationships, and my part in souring them, Beeb was having his own 'lightbulb moment'.

"My drinking... I think... is from fear," he said quietly. "Fear of the future. Fear, even, of the present."

"You've always taken the planet, and other people, to heart."

He gave a wry laugh. "The planet, yes. People less so, except in a general sense, mostly. No, Paddy, I mean fear for myself. What I'm afraid I've become. What I'm afraid I *will* become. Do you know, it's not unusual for me to feel I have to pour myself a glass of bourbon before I walk out the door to go to work in the morning? Not a shot, Paddy, a glass, like it was fruit juice, or milk. Thinking about it, I realise I'm sure other people don't need to do that to start the day. Most others. I'm afraid I don't like me very much these days."

I didn't know how to answer. Arguing with Beeb was seldom easy, or rewarding, even with a clear head. And mine certainly wasn't. But I felt that I had to try.

"I still like you."

Lame, but fundamentally honest. It won a genuine laugh.

"Thank you, my friend! But what if I asked you: why? Is it just old habit, dying hard?"

My turn to drink silently again as I considered the question.

"Respect. Admiration. For your beliefs, whether or not I agree with, or even understand all of them. For your creativity."

"Oh, Paddy, you really don't know me that well any more. I've tried, truly tried, to follow that advice you gave me a while ago about writing whenever and wherever and whatever I could. But I can never switch off the inner critic. I'll write something down, then look at it an hour, a day, a week or a month later, and pick it to pieces. Usually the page will get torn out, screwed up and thrown away. Not liking what I write; not liking me; chicken and egg."

"Do you still like the things you wrote before? When it... came easier?"

Another wry grin. "Yes. Mostly anyway. I wince at some of the less subtle bits – thank you for that insight, in case I haven't said that properly before."

"Glad to be of service," I said with a smile. "So, what's changed? What happened to the bloke who wrote that stuff you still like?"

"Things... changed. He got older, less optimistic."

"With the best will in the world, old mate, that's not a word I usually associated with you. Analytic, with a desire to be positive sometimes, but not optimistic."

"Really? I thought that's how I was. That's rather disconcerting to hear," Beeb said, more puzzled than upset.

I shrugged. "It's how you expressed yourself. Challenging people to think, not cheering them up, or on. No bad thing, I usually thought."

"I suppose you're right. To take on that role – that responsibility – requires a lot of self-confidence, though, and I don't have that any longer. The job has worn it away. I might be critical, but I don't feel challenging."

"Practicing to be a grumpy old man?" I teased.

Before Beeb could reply, a dark scrawny figure staggered up to stand between us, and draped a long hand on each of our shoulders. I turned in surprise. Under an oversized knitted Rastafarian beanie that looked like an alien lifeform swallowing his narrow head was the face of the percussionist we'd befriended at the AMUSE gig.

"Don' wanna be no grumpy ol' man, man. That ain't no fun, not for anybody."

"Good to see you, Jimmie," I said. "Been a while. Whatcha been up to?"

In truth, I had seen the Sri Lankan a few times in the years since the concert, in different bars around town. Sometimes we'd chatted, but other times he hadn't seemed to recognise me. It was a matter of what (and how much) he'd been drinking. Or otherwise consuming, I'd realised. I don't think there were many substances that Jimmie wouldn't try, or hadn't at least once.

It dawned on me that the hands on our shoulders were for his balance, as well as a show of mateship. As if the slurred voice wasn't enough of a clue, when I looked at him I realised that the whites of his eyes were mostly red. There was still something of a mischievous twinkle in the depths somewhere, but it was mostly lost among broken capillaries.

Beeb had made the same observation. "How are you, Jimmie?" he asked, concern in his voice, his introspective musings apparently vanished in an instant.

"All good, man, all good. Stayin' happy, y'know?"

"Good to hear," I replied. "You want a drink?" I asked unnecessarily.

"None for him," came a surly, unexpected voice from behind the bar. When I turned to face the barman, puzzled and annoyed, he scowled and continued, "He's already had too many."

It would not have been unreasonable to assert that the same could be said for both Beeb and I, but there seemed no reservations about plying us with more. The only obvious differences were that: Jimmie had 'loaded up' somewhere else before arriving here; he was standing (with some support, but visibly swaying) while we were perched solidly on our barstools; and his skin was a lot darker than Beeb's, mine, or the barman's.

We were prepared to get argumentative – well, I certainly was, I shouldn't speak for Beeb although I'm pretty sure we agreed on this one – but even as I opened my mouth Jimmie squeezed my shoulder and shook his head.

"Don't worry about it, man," he said with a grin. "Happens all the time. I's used to it."

Suddenly I had a mental picture of him weaving his way from bar to bar from his regular haunts on the south side, over the Victoria bridge, then in and out of a succession of city watering holes. Some of them had served him, that much was obvious.

"Never want no trouble. Youse fellas have a good afternoon, eh? I'll see you around."

"That you will, my friend," said Beeb, giving a friendly squeeze to the bony hand still on his shoulder.

"Believe it, mate," I agreed.

Jimmie gave something like an unsteady bow, then with a wave strolled back out onto Queen Street. I was in favour of downing our drinks and going with him, but Beeb cautioned against it.

"You can be sure this won't be the only bar that won't serve him.

Jimmie might be really casual about it, but I'm afraid you won't be. I'd argue, and at the very least you'd be, well, unpredictable," he pointed out.

I disagreed. "I can predict it. I'd get belligerent. It's how I'm feeling right now, and I'd only get more so with some other two-bit, jumped-up bloody Hitler…" The barman fortunately couldn't hear me, though I was glaring in his direction.

"And there's my point. Like Jimmie said, he's used to it. It's a damned shame that he has to be, but I'll take his word for it. He'd probably be embarrassed at anyone else getting into a fight on his behalf."

"Yeah, I suppose you're right," I admitted. "But I do reckon I've lost enthusiasm for drinking any more here." I threw the last of my vodka and tonic down my throat as a punctuation mark.

Beeb was more circumspect, drumming his fingertips lightly on the bar as he looked at the shallow remains of his bourbon.

"You're right, Paddy. It's not your company, my friend, but I've lost enthusiasm too. For this bar, certainly, but for drinking in general, I suddenly find. I think some of our earlier conversation has sunk in and wants me to consider it for a while."

"Well, they say the first step in overcoming a problem is recognising that there is one. Doesn't matter what I think, or anybody else. If you reckon you've got an issue, then you have. Don't know that I can be much help, but if you think of something I might do, all you've got to do is ask."

Not for a moment did I feel any sense of hypocrisy in my offering to assist with someone else's drinking problem. I hadn't acknowledged the extent of my own issues to myself. Conscious of some consequences in unguarded moments, but not really admitting there was a problem. Beeb was ahead of me in self-awareness.

"Thank you," he replied, and finished off the last skerrick of bourbon.

We stood, wavering uncertainly for a moment. Less precarious than Jimmie had been, but a noticeable degree of wobbly in our boots. A supportive hand on each other's shoulder, we walked out of the Queen Street Bar without a backward glance at the barman who'd earned our scorn. I'm sure he didn't miss us, either.

"Think I'll head home," said Beeb. "I've got things to think about. Thanks for your company today, Paddy. Not quite 'just like old times', but I've enjoyed it."

"You're more than welcome, old mate," I replied. "I've enjoyed your company, too."

What started as a handshake turned into an un-self-conscious hug before we turned and ambled off in opposite directions. Beeb presumably to enjoy, or not, an evening of quiet introspection; me to drop in to another bar for 'one more for the road' before catching a train home to a night of probably mindless television.

As I made my way along the Mall I heard music coming from the open door of a shop. The radio, I guessed, a station that specialized in the hits of ten years ago and beyond. Almost unconsciously I sang along, the tune and lyrics staying in my head long after the store was behind me and I'd settled down to another vodka and tonic.

It was Ringo Starr's *It Don't Come Easy*.

15

———

BEREAVED

Another year or so had passed when I was at my desk, irritated by yet another distraction from yet another deadline.

"Yes, who is it?" I snapped down the phone.

"My name is Michael Michaels. I'm a personnel officer in the Department of Admin Services."

"What can I do for you?" I asked, my irritation giving way to puzzlement.

"Well, ah... I'm sorry, this is very awkward. There's been an accident involving one of our staff. Mr. Brandon Bowmore. Are you a friend of...?"

"Yeah," I replied quietly. "We... go back a long way. What's happened?"

"I'm terribly sorry about this. We have no record of a next of kin, no contact number on file in case of emergency. Er, not something we check on quite as assiduously as we should, I'm afraid. All we've had to go on is Mr. Bowmore's address book in his desk drawer. Most of the few entries in it are publishing houses or interstate addresses I'm afraid. You're one of the very few local individuals listed, so I thought

I'd take a chance on calling you. Actually, you're the first whose number is still answering or even connected..."

I suppose I wasn't surprised to find he'd dropped out of touch with the handful of other friends he'd had.

"You mentioned an accident?" I prompted Michaels.

"Er, yes. Mr. Bowmore's been taken to the Royal Brisbane Hospital."

Ten minutes in a cab later I met Michael Michaels at the RBH. He seemed an unlikely personnel officer - a bearded Londoner with an earring and a blonde ponytail. He appeared genuinely agitated. I wasn't sure at first if his concern was for Beeb or just the inconvenience he'd been put to, but I admit I warmed to him quite quickly.

Over cups of dreadful machine-generated coffee, he explained what had happened. Beeb - Mr. Bowmore - had been kneeling at an open tall Stores cupboard, picking up a ream of paper from near ground level. An idiot pushing a filing trolley at high speed had collided with the rear of the cupboard. A full box of several thousand paper clips was jolted off the top shelf and crashed down on top of Beeb's head. The impact had dropped him like a school port.

We talked for a while of Beeb himself. Michael scarcely knew him - he was a name on a personnel file, but it seemed nobody in Beeb's unit was sufficiently close to him, or 'available', to make the trip to the hospital. His supervisor was "extremely busy", so it fell to Michael to take care of things.

A pretty brunette in a white coat came over to where we sat. Expecting a nurse, I was surprised by the nametag that identified her as a doctor. I remember her first name was Margaret, and that she had beautiful eyes. It's funny what sticks in your mind at stressful moments. She was young enough that I almost asked if she'd studied with Marie Hooker.

"You're friends of Mr. Bowmore?" she asked.

Michael shifted uncomfortably. I was looking at Margaret's eyes as I nodded.

"I'm sorry," she continued. "He never regained consciousness."

Clair de Lune was playing in the background. The piano suddenly seemed distant and tinny.

"A box of paper clips?" It was my voice. It must have been me speaking, although I wasn't fully conscious of it.

"A heavy box, apparently," Margaret observed. "It looks as though he was struck by the corner of the box - a penetrating blow."

Over the following days Michael went well beyond what I'm sure were the parameters of his job, helping me to arrange Beeb's cremation and service.

We had a notice placed in both the *Courier-Mail* and my own local paper, with some more details this time, and I hoped, a touch of sincere regret.

Realising that there was nobody else to take on the task, I requested some time off work and set about clearing out Beeb's home.

I hadn't visited there since school days. Structurally it hadn't changed, but it was much more spartan than I remembered. His parents' art collection was mostly gone, gifted or sold over the years I suspected. There were few adornments on the walls now. A few movie posters, among them *Casablanca* and *2001: A Space Odyssey*, and two framed autographed pictures – the unlikely pair of H. G. Wells and Chuck Berry.

The door to what had been the parental bedroom was still closed after all the time since their deaths. The bed was still made, some knick-knacks on the bedside tables with a clock that had wound down soon after their passing, and never since been touched. The wardrobes were empty, the clothes having long ago gone to Lifeline or somewhere like that. Beeb's own clothes would be similarly passed on soon enough. There was a modest layer of dust all about the room. I suspected it was cleaned a couple of times per year, perhaps as a part of a regular routine of maintenance.

The rest of the house was obviously looked after more often, if not quite meticulously.

The kitchen was by far the cleanest part of the place. Beeb hadn't lost his appreciation of good food. It was well equipped with good quality utensils and appliances. Not a lot, certainly no more than a single man required, and none of it bought because it was fashionable or The Next Big Thing, but *good*. There were a couple of items I claimed for myself, like an electric frypan and some knives which were of vastly better quality than I'd been making do with since I left home. Michael Michaels turned out to be something of a connoisseur of decent food too, and I was happy to let him take a number of items when he came to help on the weekend.

One bedroom, apparently used as a meditation room, had the old silk parachute suspended from the ceiling. The room was smaller than the lounge of the old house where I'd first encountered it, so the effective height was even lower. I doubt that anyone taller than five feet could have stood upright without getting entangled in the fabric. Where Beeb had settled in the room was indicated by a well-worn beanbag near the doorway. Beside that was a carved incense burner, with the ashes of numerous sticks still piled on it, and an old cassette player that probably dated back to our school days. All of the tapes stacked beside it were of instrumental music, from several different countries.

Against one wall were propped several books – philosophies and scriptures of a variety of cultures and denominations, as broad a mix as the origins of the music in the room. Although how he could have read much in there by the light of the red bulb suspended above the parachute, was beyond me.

There were more books in what I took to be Beeb's own bedroom (a safe guess, based on the wardrobe full of his clothes). Many of these were volumes of poetry, and again, they'd come from different cultures. Quite a few were Indian or Hindi, and judging by their age I had a hunch they were from the time when Priti had been a significant part of his life. The bed was neatly made. Presumably he'd done this every morning before going to work. I did the same, sort of, but my effort of dragging the sheet up to approximately the level of the pillows looked pretty shoddy alongside Beeb's neat folds and tucks.

There was a little square table by the bed. On it were the usual accoutrements – a clock, a glass, a pen and a notebook. The latter I was pleased to see, remembering my advice to him to keep such an item handy for preserving flashes of inspiration. I couldn't resist flicking through it. Only a few pages had been filled, and too many of those had a big X through most of their contents. Some looked promising, or interesting, or even whimsical. But the only one that jumped from the page to my eyes was a page which held only one sentence: *When did my life become so small?* I closed the notebook with something like a shudder, tried to shut down my emotions and went back to the task at hand.

A big old tallboy stood against the wall opposite the window, the heavy curtains of which were closed. It was probably the oldest piece of furniture in the house. T-shirts occupied the top drawer. The next one down evidently did service as a filing cabinet of sorts, filled with receipts, bank statements, warranties and User Guides. The middle drawer held stationery, pens, rulers, paper and notepads. The bottom two drawers of the unit were the most tightly packed, crammed with writing pads and notebooks, all of them full of Beeb's neat copper-plate handwriting, and folders full of typewritten pages. Here was where he'd stored the sum total of his creative output – those efforts that had survived the self-critical 'culls' he'd admitted to me.

There was still plenty of it. I carefully bundled it all up and secured it in a couple of plastic tubs to keep out moisture and marauding insects. My intention was, sometime soon, to read it all, edit as and if necessary, and do my damnedest to get the best of it published. And I still intend to do that sometime soon. In my own defence, and Beeb's, part of the delay has been that when I *have* read his work it's inspired me to work on some creative writing of my own, putting the editing aside for 'another day'.

The lounge room was pretty austere. There was a modestly sized television, with a video player attached. As I'd expect, a good stereo system with turntable and cassette deck sat on top of a record cabinet crammed with albums: blues, jazz, 'progressive' rock, and pretty much nothing that could be called 'pop' except a couple of early Beatles' LPs.

The seating options were a couch and a single armchair, both upholstered in Mission Brown corduroy that I was pretty sure hadn't been the choice of the artistic elder Bowmores. I suspected that this suite was a relic of days as a struggling student after his parents' passing, when the good furniture was sold off and replaced with much cheaper alternatives, and the difference was applied to the cost of living.

Between the seat options was a substantial side table that, judging by telltale stains and the half-full bourbon bottle, usually did service as Beeb's dining table. Flanking the television were two more bookshelves, these mostly given over to fiction. Much of it was fantasy and SF, with one shelf of humour – Spike Milligan, P. G. Wodehouse, Jerome K. Jerome and Douglas Adams.

The bulk of the book collection, though, was in what had once been a dining room adjoining the kitchen. Every wall of this room was now occupied by bookshelves, which even covered over the only window. They were as organized as a good public library. Different branches of science, philosophy, comparative religion, arcana, history of various countries and eras. One entire bookcase holding nothing but biographies. An old wheeled butler's trolley in the middle of the room was evidently used for sorting purposes – it was the only furniture in the room other than the bookcases. Michael whistled at the impressive array.

"Has he read all of them, do you reckon?" he asked me softly. The similarity to a library was striking enough for us to automatically lower our voices.

"Probably, over the years," I replied. "I'm sure some of them belonged to his parents, but he'd have read them anyway."

The Personnel officer examined one particular shelf. "There's some really good books on photography here," he said admiringly.

"A hobby of yours?" I asked.

"An interest, yeah. I wish I'd known it was something we shared.

But then, I really didn't know much about Brandon at all. He was a name on a file, mostly."

After all this time, it felt odd for me to hear Beeb called by his given name. It took me a moment to reply, "Don't take it to heart, mate. Very few people really knew him. That was his preference for a long time. I think the photography was more his father's thing, in any case. But I'm sure he could have had a good conversation about it!"

Michael smiled at the thought.

Among the things I found in the bedroom drawer 'filing system' was Beeb's Will. Typical of him to have been so organized, I figured, mentally promising myself to write such a document too. A promise I duly kept, several years later. Beeb's was straightforward but a little surprising.

The Public Trustee was named as Executor, for simplicity's sake rather than any abiding faith in their competence, I suspect. The house itself was to go to a charity for the homeless. If they couldn't use it directly, they were to sell it and make use of the proceeds. Most of the rest of his estate was to be similarly sold off and applied to a literacy foundation – it wouldn't amount to much. He was debt-free, but largely free of assets, too. His bank account would cover the funeral with a bit left over, there was the car (no longer worth much more than scrap value) and the basic furniture. His main expenditure had been books, and they were to be mine, to my surprise. Suddenly I had a library!

The first thing I did after that realization was to invite Michael Michaels to help himself to whatever books on photography he was interested in. I was finding his help and support invaluable, and figured he should see some reward for his efforts.

There would be a logistical problem for me, I knew that. My own book collection was already substantial, and now the numbers were about to increase fivefold. Even if I ruthlessly culled Beeb's books, selling or gifting all that I didn't have an immediate pressing interest in, I'd still be more than doubling the number I possessed. And that sort of culling didn't appeal to me. My tastes weren't dissimilar to Beeb's, although I wasn't quite as voracious a reader, and I knew that there was little in his collection I'd be completely dismissive of. There was a lot of potentially valuable research and reference material, too, for that nebulous 'one of these days' when I'd write something with more depth than a suburban news story. The problem was, where to put it all? The flat that I currently called home was already packed to the gunwales with my own reading matter. There was simply no room for what I now suddenly came into possession of.

Well, I figured, my lease didn't have long to run anyway. The Public Trustee were unlikely to move very quickly, so I'd have a bit of time to find a new, bigger place. Then I could pack up both the contents of Beeb's shelves and my own stuff, and establish my new library.

Before that, though, would have to come the funeral, or some sort of service at least.

It wasn't a conversation Beeb and I had ever had, and there were no clues in his otherwise thorough Will, so somehow it fell to me to make an 'executive decision'.

Based on a passing comment that I may have imagined as much as remembered, I chose to have him cremated, rather than buried. The funeral director I'd randomly chosen from the phone book – I liked the phrasing of their ad, I think – was quietly polite and helpful. Good at his job, in other words.

Certainly not a church service. The local cemetery had a strictly non-denominational 'chapel', though even that word seemed too strong. It was simply a nice room with rows of long seats, walls painted in a soft blue, and a picture window at the end, looking out onto a little enclosed garden with a fountain. There was tea and coffee, proper Scottish shortbread and some Ladies' Auxiliary cakes in the little function room next door.

I wrote and delivered the eulogy. I'd already been to a couple of services where a disinterested priest or a celebrant who'd never met the deceased made cringe-inspiring mistakes like getting the poor bugger's name wrong (Evan, not Ewen – read your bloody notes, man!) or had ascribed faith, beliefs or character that most everyone listening knew to be fictitious (belligerent Bob was by no stretch of the imagination a 'sober, God-fearing man'). All I did was give a little bit of my mate's history, such as I knew, and told a couple of stories I knew he'd have liked. What I hoped was that anyone who attended would leave at least knowing a little more about my intensely private old friend, and appreciating him more because of it.

It was, as you'd expect, a small affair. A few people from Uni days saw this real death notice in the Courier Mail and turned up, as did a representative of our old school. Michael Michaels came, on behalf of the Department officially, but also as a kind gesture of support. Two other blokes from work, who by their names (Halloran and Knight) I realised had been with Beeb at the brothel, although neither of them had any cause to recognise me. I didn't speak much to them, diplomatically not letting the Personnel Officer beside me know where we'd met. A gangling, earnest bloke from AMUSE. Nobody from the Gospel Hall.

Seeing the guy from AMUSE prompted me to hope that Jimmie might have appeared, but I realised that there was almost no way he'd have known about what happened. Sometime later I learned a more depressing truth – Jimmie's system had shut down from the cumulative effect of all the various substances he'd poured or poked into himself for years. Not an overdose as such, I was told, but he'd died in his sleep after a typical big night out. I hope it was peaceful for him.

I'd chosen Jethro Tull's *Elegy* to play as people arrived – a brighter tune than you might expect from the title, and closed with Emerson Lake and Palmer's *Fanfare For The Common Man*. I'm not sure that anyone caught the jest. My old friend had been anything but a common man. But he had been fond of that piece of music, which is as far as anyone probably thought.

After Beeb's service, the chap from the funeral home handed me a card that had come to their office from Prithiya. Her surname was still a confounding mix of half the alphabet, but now it commenced with an A, so I presumed she'd married. It was a beautifully handwritten card, written to Beeb himself, expressing sadness and fond remembrance. I wondered what her husband, presumably the good traditional fellow his mother-in-law had wanted, would have thought of his wife's sentiment. I was pretty confident that he didn't know.

After doing my blood cell impression and circulating among the handful of people loitering over the Light Refreshments, I adjourned to a nearby bar. It wasn't a regular haunt for either of us. Indeed, I wasn't sure that Beeb had such a thing. I was pretty sure most of his drinking was done at home in the past few years. But it was conveniently located for this day. I'd quietly let it be known that this was the plan, and anyone who wanted to come along, raise a glass and even swap a story or memory of Brandon Baxter Bowmore was very welcome. Three or four did so, at least briefly.

Michael Michaels was able to fit in one drink before having to return to his office, a couple of the ex-Uni folks did likewise. Angela had sent her apologies and sincere sympathies. She'd had genuinely fond memories of Beeb, but her Public Service career was continuing its steep upward trajectory and there was an important meeting she was expected to chair, sure I'd understand? I did, in my own way.

As the last of the 'stayers' nodded and smiled and slipped out of the bar, in walked Eric 'Fish' Jones, rather more than fashionably late.

I bit down on saying, "So you've been allowed out," but that was exactly the phrase he then used himself.

He'd been 'allowed out' by Penny when he'd explained the situation, having missed the funeral itself through a combination of work and marital disapproval ("But that's one of your busiest, best-paying times of the week!", which was sad but true. He did have a large mortgage to pay.)

"How is married life, mate?" I asked.

"It's a life of constant adjustment. For both of us. There's the bloke Penny wants me to be. There's the bloke I have to be with my patients. There's the bloke I used to be hanging around with you guys."

"Which one's the real Eric Jones?"

"Bit of all of them, I suppose. Or a bit of him is in all of 'em. No girlfriend or partner for Beeb at the end, I take it?" he asked, with a small but deft redirection of the subject.

I shook my head. "Not really since soon after we left school. He was close to a girl for a time then, but when that got scuppered by her mother, well, it's like he never really looked again."

"That's a shame. He did always seem content in his own company, I guess."

"Yeah," I answered vaguely, remembering more recent encounters with Beeb that belied that observation, or at least dated it.

"What about you?" Fish asked affably. "I know there's nobody here with you, but where are you at?"

"Between engagements," I replied, conscious of the optimistic pun.

"Weren't you and Ange living together?"

"Yeah, but that sort of fell apart, quite a while ago. Incompatible ambitions."

He looked at me in puzzlement.

"I didn't have any," I explained. "Pretty much still don't, really. Just drifting along, day to day. Much like Beeb was doing the last couple of years..." I said the last bit quietly, the thought addressed to myself as much as Fish.

"Mm. That's not so good, mate. Not if you aren't enjoying it – and, sorry, you don't sound like you are."

I smiled, appreciating the sympathy both for the loss of an old friend, and my own depression – more evident than I'd realised.

Fish continued. "At least I get to feel like I'm doing some good for people sometimes. They don't all deserve it. There's some right nanas among my patients, but I've gotta treat 'em all alike and hope they get better, in more ways than one."

"Good attitude, old mate! I reckon my doctor thinks on similar lines. Last time I saw him, he told me I was in pretty fair shape for a forty-five-year-old."

"But you're only... ah! I get it! Shrewd fella. So, have you taken the hint?" he asked, putting on his best Serious Doctor's face.

"Not really, I'm afraid. Bit light on in the motivation department. It's just a phase. I'll get over it."

Fish nodded uncertainly, but diplomatic enough to again shift the subject. We talked a bit about old times. Recalled the days of flagons and wine casks chilling in the lake, and he talked about the much better standard of wines he was drinking these days. I'd been mostly sticking to spirits in the last few years, but his enthusiastic descriptions piqued my interest, and I resolved to try a few things. I knew a good bottle shop not far out of town that had a tasting table set up every Saturday afternoon. I'd seen it but never indulged.

He also told me about a regular monthly champagne tasting evening at a nice bar in the Valley that sounded appealing. Not cheap, but interesting, good quality stuff being showcased every month. The woman running it wasn't at all snobby, he reckoned, just knew and loved good champagne and wanted to educate and share her passion with others. Good idea, I thought.

"See you at next month's tasting, maybe?" I wondered out loud.

"That'd be good. They're an outing Penny approves of – she's fond of bubbles herself," he said wryly.

"Maybe best not to warn her I might be there, eh? I'll try to be circumspect and behave myself." My tongue was planted firmly in my cheek, but we shared a conspiratorial laugh.

A drink or two later, he had to be on his way. But by then my mood was a bit lighter. Still grieving, but better. I realised that my grief wasn't really for Beeb. I'd miss him, but he hadn't suffered. Not in death, anyway. It was too quick for that. His suffering had been the last years of his life: unsatisfied, unsatisfying, directionless. And my real grieving was for myself and the realization that I was trudging along the same path.

Fish had given me a nudge, both as a friend and as a medical professional who took his calling more seriously than anyone had expected. I parked the dawning new thoughts at the back of my mind, the better for them to gestate.

A little while later I laid Beeb's ashes to rest in the garden of the house I soon rented in Tarragindi – a big enough place to accommodate our combined book collection. It seemed a small way to acknowledge his deep care for the environment. I planted a small *Leptospermum laevigatum* over them.

That 'coastal tea tree' has grown into a handsome bush that I still admire whenever I pass my old address. Seeing it conjures a small flood of images and I can't help but smile. It's not 'wallowing in the past', I truly believe that. It's reflecting, trying to learn.

What did Beeb ever teach me? An echo sounded in my head, the first time I stuck that little shrub into the dirt. "I'm afraid I don't like me very much anymore." I was disconcerted to realise I felt the same way. Realise it at last.

One of the first of my newly-acquired books that I'd opened was a book of African tribal proverbs and philosophies. One that had jumped out at me was roughly translated as: "*It does not matter to be a successful person – it matters to be a person of value*". That resonates for me. My kind of ambition.

Maybe it's time to stop closing myself off behind the wall of alcohol. Probably never quit drinking, I admit, but I know I've wound it back. I can wind it back some more.

Maybe I'll start thinking about relationships seriously again - find somebody I can offer more to than some laughs and lightweight conversation. Rediscover the hopeless romantic inside me that I'd thought I'd drowned.

Maybe I'll try my hand at writing more than *This Week In Your Suburb*. Deeper than "an enthusiastic crowd of nearly twenty enjoyed the Buffalos' gutsy effort at Stunden Oval..." More memorable than "Mrs. Dundee is proud to have won Best In Show at the annual Orchid Society display for the third year in a row..." Something I can actually enjoy and be proud of, not just be paid for.

Last time I looked at that bush, coming up healthy and strong, it conjured an unexpected thought. Funny – I don't remember us dissecting plants back at school, the way we did various critters. I'm sure we must have, they were 'biological' things that we studied, but I can't recall any details. A shame, in good old 20:20 hindsight. They've got their own life cycles, advantages, disadvantages, tough breaks, little wins. Back then, I just didn't find them interesting enough to stick in the memory. To take root – excuse the puns please, Beeb.

Ironically, I discovered a little while ago that, as popular as the coastal tea tree is in Australia, it's regarded as a much-disliked weed in South Africa. Well, Beeb was always one for polarizing opinions.

Earle Seccombe once asked the members of his Grade 12 English class what our ambitions were. Beeb's answer was simple. "I want to be remembered," he said.

He is.

ALSO BY RENOIR

<u>The *Dubious Magic* series:</u>

The Wizard Of Waramanga

The Carvings Of Cobbemarmoo

The Mad Machines of Mundara

The Warriors Of Wiwo'ole

The Spirits Of Sron Dubh

The Sailors Of Svalgsay

The Treasure Of Tepatamwa

The Masks Of Manovalo

<u>Also:</u>

For The Young And Old Souls

These Old Bastards...

After 40 Years It Gets A Bit Vague

<u>A *Quiet Word* about men's health:</u>

Mid-Life Crisis MANagement

Move It Like You Mean It - Living with Parkinsons

www.ingramcontent.com/pod-product-compliance
Lightning Source LLC
Chambersburg PA
CBHW070028120726
47909CB00003B/1096